The Aviary

Thomas Settimi

THE AVIARY

ISBN 13: 978-0692516874

Sky Scientific Press
Brookings, Oregon

Cover photo by Jorge Salcedo/Shutterstock.com

Also by Thomas Settimi . . .

CONVERGENCE
Paperback (ISBN-13: 978-1419661518)
eBook Edition 2012

ROSWELL 1947
Paperback (ISBN-13: 978-0615829173)
eBook Edition 2013

BEAK OF THE TURTLE
Paperback (ISBN-13: 978-0692210802)
eBook Edition 2014

BEYOND 2020
Paperback (ISBN-13: 978-1074544676)
eBook Edition 2019

CHAPTER ONE

Cedarpines Park, California
Christmas Eve 1964

"JUST RELAX, JASON, I can take care of these few dishes." Pamela Devereux rose from the kitchen table, carrying away the plates and empty soup bowls from lunch she had prepared for herself and her grandson.

"Toss me that dishtowel, Grandma. You wash, I'll dry." Pamela smiled as she gently released the soiled spoons and dishes into the sudsy water in the left side of sink, then reached for the white towel nearby and held it up for her grandson as he rose from the table to join her at the sink.

The old house was built in 1939 by Pamela's late husband, Bertrand. It stood at the edge of town on a parcel of land that was originally subdivided into dozens of 25-foot wide lots. The developer hoped to make a pile of money by offering the small plots to residents of Los Angeles and environs for weekend camping escapes from the bustle of the city.

When the properties attracted few takers, Bertrand was able to purchase eight of the lots for just a few hundred dollars and recombine them for a home site.

From the kitchen window one could look out over a large wood deck at the rear of the house and the forest of pine trees and scattered oaks beyond. What was once a functioning aviary at the edge of the deck had fallen into total disrepair; the wood framework long since turned to a weathered gray and the door and much of the chicken wire missing.

Pamela often spent hours looking out on the deck as dozens of feathered visitors came and went, attracted by the bowls of fresh water and wild birdseed that she refilled almost daily. As they tended to the lunch dishes, Pamela and Jason watched as a pair of Steller's Jays chased away several of the smaller colored finches.

"Have you heard from your brother?" Pamela's voice was shrill with worry. She continued, "I watch the evening news—so many boys killed over there each week. I wish that damn war would come to an end. I know you must be worried about him."

Robert was Jason's younger half-brother, six years younger than Jason, but they grew up together in their mother's home in San Diego. Jason's parents separated shortly after he was born, and his mother later remarried. When not in school, the boys would often spend time with Jason's grandparents in the mountains.

Neither of Robert's grandmothers was still living and Pamela was "Grandma" to both boys.

"No, I've heard nothing since his unit shipped out. I write, but he doesn't answer. He must still be pissed off at me."

The war in Vietnam had intensified over the last year and Robert enlisted in the Army earlier that summer, the day after his eighteenth birthday. In contrast, Jason had avoided military service entirely by qualifying for a student deferment as a college undergraduate. When he learned that he wouldn't be eligible for another draft deferment as an engineering graduate student, he interviewed and was offered a job at the Air Force Weapons Laboratory in Albuquerque—a defense-related civil service position that qualified him for an occupational deferment.

Military service had been a long tradition in the Devereux family. Grandfather Bertrand served in France during World War I and Anton Devereux—Jason's father—joined the RAF in 1940 as a member of the American Eagle Squadron, more than a year before America entered the war. Robert could not understand why his older brother chose not to carry on his own family's military tradition and it had strained the relationship between the brothers.

As Pamela added the dried dishes to a stack on the cupboard shelf, she paused momentarily, taking note of some new activity near the aviary. A young Rock Pigeon—dark gray with an iridescent purple neck—alighted on the deck railing near the open door to the aviary, setting the pair of jays to flight in the direction of the forest.

"Isn't that the same pigeon that was here yesterday? The markings look the same," remarked Jason.

"He's been coming by every day about this time for the last week." Pamela continued, "You know, when your father was a boy he raised pigeons with your grandfather. It was one of the few things they had in common. There was one very special pigeon. But for that bird, you might have never known your father."

CHAPTER TWO

RAF Base Catterick,
North Yorkshire, England
May 1940

"YANK OR CANUCK?" Squadron Leader Jeremy Wright was interviewing the pilot training candidate, a recent arrival from North America. The results of the dozen interviews he would conduct on this day would determine each candidate's future service assignment. A select few would become trainees for coveted Fighter Command duties, but most would end up in Coastal Command, eventually to patrol the North Atlantic or North Sea waters off the British Isles.

"Does it matter?" Anton Devereux understood that it was in his best interest to show a more circumspect attitude toward the Squadron Leader, but he was exhausted, having slept little during the long flight from Newfoundland.

"Yes it does, Mister..." Squadron Leader Wright glanced down at the notepad where he had moments earlier scribbled this candidate's name, "... Mister Devereux. Should it become necessary to return your remains to your loved ones back home, we want to be sure to have the correct flag on your coffin."

"Sorry, sir," Anton paused before continuing, "I'm American, from California."

"Very good, Mister Devereux." The Squadron Leader sorted through the stack of file folders on his desk until he found the one marked 'USA'. Anton Devereux's application for service in the RAF was the first one in the folder. "It says here that you received flight training at Hancock Flight School in California and that you hold a commercial pilot license issued by the CAA in 1937. Is that correct?"

"Correct. I passed with the highest score in my class for both the written and flying portions of the exam."

"Thank you for that, Mister Devereux, but there are a few additional items that I need to verify." Squadron Leader Wright continued, "You are unmarried?"

"Yes."

It wasn't technically correct. Anton and his wife separated after six months of marriage, just a few weeks after their son Jason was born, but no divorce papers had yet been filed. Their friends were surprised that the marriage lasted as long as it did as the couple appeared to have very little in common. When Anton completed his application for the American Eagle Squadron before leaving California, he marked his marital status as "single" because he knew that the RAF would accept only unmarried applicants.

Anticipating the Squadron Leader's next questions, he quickly added, "and I've logged more than 300 flight hours—mainly crop dusting. Also, I am slightly near-sighted," Anton tapped the eyeglass case in his shirt pocket, "but my corrected vision is 20/20. I had hoped to sign up with the U.S. Army Air Corps, but as I'm sure you know, they require perfect uncorrected vision. Besides, I didn't have the required two years of university study."

Squadron Leader Wright made a notation on Anton's application and returned it to the file folder. Leaning back in his chair, he posed one more question to the candidate, "What is it you are trying to accomplish here, Mister Devereux?"

"My family has a history of fighting Germans. My grandfather was wounded in the Ardennes Forest, and at least one distant Devereux relative fought in the Franco-Prussian War. Even if America gets into this war someday, my eyesight makes me ineligible to fly for my country. The RAF is my best chance to fight, doing what I know best, and even that wouldn't have possible until recently."

It was true. It would be another eighteen months before America joined the Allies in the War in Europe and early participation by individual Americans was restricted. Officially, the Neutrality Laws passed by Congress and a

Presidential Proclamation issued on September 5, 1939, specifically prohibited U.S. citizens from serving in the military organization of any combatant nation. The creation of the American Eagle Squadron and similar initiatives to place American pilots in service with the RAF were seemingly in direct violation of these strict neutrality regulations. Unofficially, the initiatives were supported by the Roosevelt Administration and the Justice Department was urged to simply ignore most suspected violations.

Upon hearing the distinctive sound of an aircraft engine throttling down, the men turned to watch as a Supermarine Spitfire gracefully touched down on the grass landing strip. Anton pointed and exclaimed, "I want to fly one of those!" They watched until the pilot secured the engine and climbed out of the cockpit.

Turning back to the matter at hand, the Squadron Leader announced, "You will be pleased to learn, Mister Devereux, that I am recommending you for Fighter Command flight training. But understand that it will be some time before you find yourself behind the controls of a Spitfire. Here at Catterick, you will train in one of our Brewster Buffaloes, generously provided by the U.S. Government."

THE OLD BELL TAVERN in North Yorkshire was a popular watering hole for British pilots and the relatively few members of the American Eagle Squadron. But by early 1942, the number of American patrons began to steadily increase.

Anton Devereux sat quietly nursing a beer at the bar, ignoring the airman sitting on the barstool next to him until he heard the man order another drink.

"You're an American," said Anton. The man turned toward Anton.

"Yes, I am. The name is Ken Stone. What's yours?" Stone extended his right hand and Anton reciprocated.

"Anton Devereux, RAF. Are you new to Catterick?"

"New, yes, but I'm headed to Ridgewell. My bomber group arrived from the States yesterday."

"B-17s, right? It's a good thing that British Bomber Command will finally have some worthy competition," said Anton. Ken Stone chuckled at Anton's remark.

"So what do you fly, Anton?"

"Spitfire for now, but it wasn't always the case. We trained for a few months in Brewster Buffaloes—probably the worst airplane ever produced for the U.S. Army Air Corps. The Army pawned them off on the Brits and they returned the favor by using them as trainers for new RAF pilots. I'm told that some of the boys who got here before me even flew a few combat missions with that plane. Eventually, they were replaced by Hawker Hurricanes and Spitfires, but not until the pilots figured out they could induce a ground loop by 'forgetting' to lock the tail wheel on landing. The damaged planes were scrapped and—thankfully—replaced with the Hawkers."

Anton and Ken Stone became friends. On several occasions, Anton's fighter group was assigned escort duty for bombing raids conducted by Ken's 381st Bomb Group. During the return leg to England Anton would often maneuver his Spitfire to a safe distance near the underside of the B-17 *"Big Time Operator"* and exchange a salute with Ken Stone, the Ball Turret Gunner.

CHAPTER THREE

Berlin, Germany
October 1921

WERNHER'S FATHER, MAGNUS, had set up the small refractor telescope—a gift from Wernher's mother—inside the garden of the large family estate. In less than a minute the young boy had the scope trained and focused on the first quarter moon in the western sky; the image nearly filling the entire field of view through the telescope.

From an early age, Wernher's keen interest in science—especially astronomy—was encouraged by his parents. Magnus had been a Minister of Agriculture in the Federal Cabinet of the Weimar Republic. The move to Berlin to take a civil service position in the Department of Interior would provide the best opportunity for Wernher and his two brothers to receive a proper quality education.

"Do you see, Father, the division between the dark and lighted half of the surface?" Magnus had taken a turn at the eyepiece. The young boy continued, "It's called the *terminator*. It's where the sun is setting on the surface. The mountains and craters stand out more because of the long shadows." Magnus smiled to himself. He was proud that he had learned a new fact from his nine year-old son.

The lunar image drifted from the field of view after a minute or two and Wernher took another turn at the eyepiece, repositioning the telescope. He mused, "Do you believe that humans will ever walk on the moon, Father?"

"I don't know, Wernher. What do you think?"

WHILE ATTENDING BOARDING SCHOOL near Weimar, Wernher was given a copy of *By Rocket into Interplanetary Space* by the famous rocket pioneer, Hermann Oberth. That book was singularly instrumental in shaping the life and career of Wernher von Braun for the next fifty years.

Von Braun earned a doctorate in physics from the University of Berlin in 1934, studying under a research grant from the German Army. At the time, Germany was still attempting to project the illusion that it was in compliance with the terms of Treaty of Versailles negotiated at the close of World War I. While there was a prohibition on establishing an air force, it was not surprising that the 1919 treaty document made no mention of rocket or missile-related initiatives. The subject of von Braun's doctoral thesis was liquid-fueled rockets, and he subsequently became Technical Director of the Peenemünde Army Research Center on the

Baltic Sea where development of the V-2 ballistic missile began in earnest. Until the outbreak of war in 1939, the German rocket scientists frequently consulted with the American rocket pioneer, Robert Goddard.

There has been much speculation regarding von Braun's affiliation with the Nazi Party before and during the war. Party membership was expected for every high ranking official in Hitler's important weapons programs, and von Braun applied for membership and was accepted in 1937. When asked years later about his Nazi Party affiliation he stated that he had joined because refusal to do so would have meant giving up his life's work. He offered a similar explanation when asked why he had accepted an honorary rank in a branch of the SS—the infamous Nazi *Schutzstaffel* paramilitary organization.

CHAPTER FOUR

Near Noyon, France
(West of Reims)
August 1943

MICHEL DEPIERRE confronted the explosives specialist, first grasping the young man by both shoulders and then pushing him backwards. He chided, "Two fuse failures in two days. What's the problem, Francois?" The engine and flat cars of the ammunition train from Stuttgart should have been reduced to wreckage, broken and on fire on both sides of the track. Instead, the unscathed train continued toward Rouen, the engineer and army guards aboard unaware of the destructive plot that nearly befell them.

"*Desole*—I'm sorry, Michel. The fuse should have set off the Plastique just as the coal car passed over the charge." The electrical fuse that Francois designed was supposed to close a spring-loaded switch after first contact with the locomotive's forward driving wheel, initiating a short delay before the completed battery circuit set off the charge. "I know the switch works; it must be my delay circuit." Michel and the other two members of team stood with arms folded in front of them as Francois offered his apologetic explanation.

Michel and Francois were the last members to join this French Resistance cell, first organized in the weeks following the country's surrender and signing of the Armistice with Germany in June 1940. The cell had spent the last two years successfully harassing the occupying Germans by blowing up fuel and ammunition depots and the occasional power plant.

The group had purposely ruled out direct assassination of German soldiers or officials as Nazi retribution in such cases was both swift and brutal. On more than one occasion, the SS responded to the murder of a German officer or bureaucrat by taking eighty or more French citizens from the nearest town as hostages and then shooting them in the street. The train attacks were a new initiative for the team, considered only recently as they had destroyed—or at least attempted to destroy— most of the less well-protected stationary targets in the surrounding region.

"Do we dare retrieve the package?" Michel knew the answer to his question before he asked it.

"A dud is a dud until it blows up in someone's face. We have to leave it," offered Francois, "I don't trust my delay circuit after today."

A PAIR OF FIGHTER AIRCRAFT screamed at treetop level above the team of four as they headed toward their home village of Noyon. The sight of the swastika on the tails and the *Balkenkreuz* on the underside of the wings caused the team members to drop to the ground, seeking cover. A new sound was added seconds later, even before the low-flying Messerschmitts disappeared behind the tree line. Two Mark V Spitfires were in hot pursuit of the German planes, their V-12 Rolls-Royce Merlin engines at full throttle. The Messerschmitts reappeared to the men on the ground as the German aircraft began a steep rolling climb, separating from one another.

The team on the ground watched in amazement as the adversaries in the sky engaged in a classic dogfight with barrel rolls, Immelmann turns and other assorted aerobatics. Machine gun tracer fire crisscrossed the deep blue sky as the planes maneuvered about, each side seeking an offensive advantage.

When one of the German planes exploded in a ball of orange flame, his partner disengaged and headed for safety in the East, apparently failing to notice the stream of smoke trailing the British aircraft he had been pursuing. The team on the ground heard the Spitfire's engine sputter and die and then saw a lone white parachute billow open a thousand feet above them. They rushed toward the pilot as his feet touched down in a clearing only fifty yards away, his chute collapsing as it drifted to the ground. The second Spitfire circling high overhead now headed west with wings wagging, signifying to the downed pilot that he had been seen, apparently secure for now on the ground below.

The team leader was the first to speak with the downed pilot, "My name is Michel Depierre, and we are with the Resistance. Welcome to France."

The young flyer replied, "I am Anton Devereux. *Vive la France.*"

CHAPTER FIVE

Cedarpines Park, California
Christmas Eve 1964

"IT WAS YOUR FATHER'S COAT, but it seems to fit you just fine." Pamela Devereux gazed at her grandson for a moment, reflecting on how much the young man resembled her son, Anton. As he stood at the doorway, she stepped on to the deck and set the two cups of hot tea on the small glass table between the lounge chairs. It was cold and clear and as they sipped, the late afternoon sun felt good on their faces. They sat silently together, relishing the view of the forest and the sound of the brisk wind whistling through the pine branches. After several minutes, Pamela finally responded to a question Jason had asked earlier in the kitchen, "Your father just didn't want to talk about the War."

"I know that. He would change the subject whenever I asked him about it. I just never understood why."

"Well, you were only—what—ten years old when he returned from the war?" Jason nodded. "And he left again after only three years. Maybe he thought you were just too young. He witnessed some pretty terrible things, you know. Sometimes when he couldn't sleep he'd come down to the kitchen. I'd find him there in the early morning and sit with him at the table. He'd just start talking about it—I didn't even have to ask."

Jason frowned and decided to change the subject. "So you were saying earlier that when his plane was shot down, he was rescued by some Frenchmen?"

"Yes. That's what they told us. When that brown Army car drove up to the house and the two men in uniform came to the door, I expected to hear the worst. They told us your father's fighter squadron was escorting British bombers that day when the German planes attacked and his plane was hit. When he bailed out, the pilot of the other Spitfire circled overhead until he saw that your father was safely on the ground. From that other pilot's report, the Army believed that members of the French Underground rescued your father, but of course they couldn't be certain.

"Officially, he was considered 'Missing in Action' until it could be confirmed, but the Army was hopeful. The French Underground helped many downed RAF pilots get back to England during the war. Your grandfather and I waited to hear the good news—and eventually any news at all—about your father, but we heard nothing. Maybe he had been captured by the Germans and would be released when the war ended, but eventually we gave up all hope of ever seeing our son again. It was 1950—eight years after your father disappeared—before we learned what happened to him."

CHAPTER SIX

Peenemünde, on the Baltic Sea
August 1943

THE WAR HAD BEEN GOING BADLY for Germany for more than a year. In North Africa, Rommel was defeated at El Alamein, and on the Eastern Front, the Sixth Army was stopped at Stalingrad. Nearly every major city in Germany had suffered under frequent British and American bombing raids. Desperate for any initiative that might reverse the course of the War, the German High Command began to pour more resources into weapons development. The unmanned "buzz bomb" and A4 ballistic missile had been redesignated as V-weapons for *vergeltung* or "vengeance" at the urging of propaganda minister Goebbels.

The first V-1 attacks on London would not occur until June 1944, with operational V-2 launches commencing three months later. The V-1 was a subsonic, unmanned, air-breathing aircraft—a precursor to the modern day cruise missile. More than 9,000 V-1s were fired at Britain from launch sites on the French coast.

Although most of the missiles were downed by antiaircraft fire or RAF interceptors, those that got through the defenses caused some 6,000 deaths and three times as many injuries in London alone. Antwerp, Belgium, became the target of V-1 attacks after the French launch sites were disrupted following the Allied D-Day invasion.

The V-2 was a 12-ton rocket using liquid oxygen and alcohol as the propellant. Both the V-1 and V-2 missiles carried a one-ton conventional warhead, but the V-2 had a greater range and could not be intercepted due to its high terminal velocity—nearly 4,000 miles per hour—before impact.

Development and testing of the missiles at the Peenemünde Army Research Center did not escape the attention of the Allied High Command. It was understood that once the V-weapons became operational, they would threaten not only British cities and military installations, but could interfere with the Allied invasion of France planned for the following year. There was also concern that the Nazis might use the missiles to deliver deadly Sarin gas or—although less likely—an atomic warhead or radioactive "dirty" bomb. Not until war's end was it learned that German scientists were still years away from developing an atomic weapon.

Plans for strategic bombing of Peenemünde were finalized after British Intelligence received maps and reports forwarded by spies in contact with two Polish janitors working at the Center. Nearly 600 British heavy bombers participated in the Operation Hydra raid on the evening of August 17, 1943, dropping 1,800 tons of explosives on the facilities at Peenemünde.

DIRECTOR VON BRAUN made the announcement at a meeting of his staff just two days after the British air raid. "By now you have all heard the bad news that the English bombing attack has killed Walter Thiel and Chief Engineer Walther." Thiel was von Braun's rocket engine designer. Von Braun continued, "The unfinished V-2 production area also sustained severe damage. But there is some good news to report: a new research and production facility near Nordhausen will soon be operational. It will be a deep underground facility, protected from the British and American bombs."

By October 1943 nearly all of the machinery and personnel from Peenemünde had been relocated to the Mittelwerk facility in a former gypsum mine under the Harz Mountains near Nordhausen.

CHAPTER SEVEN

Occupied France
February 1944

SIX MONTHS HAD PASSED since Anton was rescued by Michel Depierre and his Resistance Cell. Like most French Underground teams, Depierre's cell operated independently, not knowing the activities of other teams or the identity of their members. This decentralized organization was purposeful. If a member of the Resistance was captured and interrogated, only the members of his immediate cell would be at risk.

But decentralization brought with it one clear disadvantage: Michel met with his Resistance handler, known to him only as *Le Furet*—The Ferret—infrequently. It was weeks after Anton was rescued before Michel learned that two of the cells that successfully escorted downed British pilots through southern France and across the Pyrenees into Spain had been compromised by German agents posing as British flyers. It might be months before a new French "Underground Railroad" could be established allowing Anton to be repatriated back to England.

The members of the cell had gathered at a deserted farm house just outside Michel's home village of Noyon. When Michel gave Anton the bad news, the American asked, "How else can I get back to my RAF unit?"

Michel answered without looking up from the map of Europe he had unfolded on the dining table, "There are limited options. Switzerland is out. If the authorities there learned that you were flying for the RAF, you would be interred there until the end of the war. I've heard rumors that many of the internment guards are Nazi sympathizers; it might be an unpleasant experience."

"I had hoped to get back to my unit before the end of the War."

"*Le Furet* told me that three American flyers recently made their way out through Sweden. It's riskier, but certainly a possibility."

"No thanks," offered Anton. "Moving several hundred miles through occupied Belgium and the Netherlands? Not to mention northern Germany and Denmark. It would be suicide."

"There is a third option." Michel hesitated.

"Let's hear it."

"Why not work with us for a while? We could use your help, and when a safe route to Spain reopens, you can leave. It shouldn't be more than a few months—well before any end to this war."

Anton stroked his chin, thoughtfully considering Michel's suggestion.

THEY HAD REACHED their target for the evening—a wooden railroad bridge north of Reims—just after midnight. Two team members nearby were acting as lookouts, hiding in the woods, one each north and south of the bridge and just off the unpaved road that ran parallel to the tracks. Girard, the fifth member of the team, waited at the far end of the bridge for a signal from Michel to light the fuse to the charge he had attached to the underside of one of the structural cross timbers. The plan was for the charges to go off simultaneously, or at least not more than a few seconds apart. The only source of illumination was the last quarter moon, now low in the western sky, and Anton could barely make out the shape of Girard, unrecognizable in the dim light ten meters away.

"I've never worked with dynamite," Anton said as Michel handed him a stick of the explosive. *Le Furet* was their source for all types of weapons and bomb-making supplies, but his stock of Plastique was low and in recent weeks only the less-popular dynamite was available.

"Just think of it as a large firecracker," Michel quipped, hoping to reduce the tension in the air.

"That doesn't help me. When I was twelve a firecracker went off in my hand before I could throw it," replied Anton. His words were barely spoken when a single shot rang out—a warning from one of the lookouts that German soldiers must be close by. Seconds later, another shot; this one from the opposite direction. Now they could see multiple lights approaching from beyond both ends of the bridge—flashlight beams directed every which way in the dark. With no place to run and clearly outnumbered, the three men hid themselves in the dense shrubbery below the bridge and waited in the dark, hoping to remain undiscovered.

The two squads of Germans coming from opposite directions met on the tracks near the middle of the bridge. They were so close that Michel and Anton could hear the officer issuing orders to his men, and the soldiers began scanning the ground below the bridge with two searchlights. Excited shouts filled the air as a single bright spotlight found Girard. He looked up, facing the spotlight momentarily before darting away—attempting to avoid the light. But the light followed his every move, and a burst of gunfire from a German Mauser stopped him. His body rolled down the rocky slope toward the ground below the middle of the bridge. Moments later a second searchlight was trained on Michel and Anton.

"*Halten Sie!* Do not move. You are under arrest." Anton searched Michel's face momentarily for a clue. What was he thinking? Should they stand and fight, or try to run or simply give up? When Michel dropped his weapon and raised his hands in surrender, Anton did the same.

THE PRISONER'S HANDS were bound in front of them and *Leutnant* Frisch and his men marched them a kilometer along the road to where the northern-most squad had left their vehicles, guarded by two soldiers. *Gefreiter* (Corporal) Schmitt folded back the canvas flap at the covered rear bed of the Opel Blitz troop carrier and motioned for the prisoners to climb aboard. Four armed soldiers with weapons ready followed the prisoners into the back of the truck and the canvas was secured. After Schmitt and the rest of the squad joined *Leutnant* Frisch in the lead vehicle, the drivers set off along the dirt road until it joined the main highway toward Compiègne.

Anton and Michel sat together on the bench up against the cab wall of the covered truck bed, heads bowed and their bound hands in their laps. They had discussed this eventuality months earlier when Anton first committed to join the Resistance Cell. The pair concluded that it would be best not to be taken alive— better to be shot while conducting an act of sabotage rather than undergoing a brutal interrogation and then face a firing squad, but that opportunity had passed.

If he were arrested, Anton even considered whether it would be best to reveal or try to conceal his true identity as an American flying for the RAF. His conclusion—and Michel agreed—was that the RAF connection would be of no help. An American pilot out of uniform would be treated as a spy, no differently than a captured Resistance fighter. Anton was fairly fluent in the language even before he was rescued by Michel's team, and now—months later—he spoke like a native Frenchman, a role he would play for his captors.

They drove for an hour before arriving at the Nazi Regional Headquarters, occupying one entire wing of the Château de Compiègne. Originally constructed as a residence for King Louis XV, the building served as an art and science museum before the German Occupation.

There was plenty of vacant space among the building's galleries as most of the paintings and sculptures had been confiscated by officials of the Third Reich. *Reichsmarschall* Hermann Göring, head of the Luftwaffe, personally earmarked a number of the pieces for delivery to Carinhall, his country residence northeast of Berlin.

The Germans had converted a bank of small offices, formerly occupied by museum officials, into makeshift holding cells for detainees. Iron bars now secured the window openings and office doors were replaced with steel-reinforced solid oak units with a slotted opening so that guards could monitor their charges. The rooms were devoid of furnishings except for a straw mattress and a bucket for toilet functions. A ceiling light fixture had been added, controlled by an on/off switch on the outside wall near the door. Anton and Michel were thrown into separate, non-adjacent "cells."

Although exhausted from the stress of events and the late hour, Anton could not sleep. He lay on his straw mattress, looking up at the dim light bulb in the ceiling, considering his predicament. He had been roughed up a bit by his captors, but was in better shape than Michel who had suffered a blow from a rifle butt when failing to respond quickly enough when asked his name. The swelling on Michel's cheekbone had nearly closed his right eye. And then, of course, there was poor Girard—a family man with small children, he was told. All in all, Anton believed he might have fared better if he had been picked up by a German patrol and taken to an internment camp rather than being rescued by Michel and members of the Resistance cell only to be arrested these few months later and probably shot for his trouble.

It was daybreak before Anton fell into a restless sleep. He awoke four hours later, startled by the clank of the lock and screech of the hinges as the door to his cell swung open. One of the guards placed a tin cup and what looked like a crust of bread on a metal plate on the floor near the doorway. The guard pointed at him and spoke, *"Fünfzehn Minuten!"* and then exited, closing and locking the cell door.

Anton's grasp of the German language was worse than weak. He wasn't sure if the guard meant *fifteen* minutes, or maybe *fifty* minutes, but he rose immediately to discover that the cup held only water, not the coffee he hoped for, and the piece of bread was so stale as to be inedible. The water at least was fresh and it quenched his thirst.

From the barred window opening he could view the courtyard below—about ten meters square. Across the courtyard were four stout posts in the ground, close to the back wall and maybe two meters high and the same distance apart. He wondered for a few seconds when prisoners were last tied to those posts, then quickly turned away in an attempt to dispel the vision of the imaginary execution from his mind.

The sound of boots in the hallway brought Anton to his cell door in time to see Michel moving past him, half supported by a guard on each side. That Michel was in pain was apparent from the expression on his face, although no new marks or bruises could be seen. They stopped two doors away, across the hall and pushed Michel into his cell, then made their way back to the door of Anton's cell.

One of guards barked an order, "*Zurückbewegen*—Move back!" and Anton obliged by moving to the center of the room. The door was opened and the guard beckoned Anton to come out into the hall.

THE INTERROGATION ROOM was windowless, but well-lighted. The guards who had brought Anton from his cell led him to the single wooden chair facing a large desk and ordered him to sit, then waited at attention—one on each side of door. It was fifteen minutes before SS *Sturmbannführer* (Major) Wetzel entered the room.

Wetzel was forty years old, jet black hair without a trace of gray, tall and ruggedly handsome. He hung his officer's cap on the coat rack behind the desk and eased himself into the leather desk chair. Without looking up at the prisoner he lit a cigarette and examined the arrest report that lay open on the desk in front of him.

Major Wetzel removed his reading glasses and looked directly at Anton. *"Sprechen Sie Deutsch?"* he asked. Anton shook his head. *"Englisch?"*

"Some English," replied Anton.

"Good. My French is terrible and my chief interpreter has been temporarily reassigned to Paris." Major Wetzel took one more draught from his cigarette and snuffed it out in the ashtray. He continued, "Your identification papers list your name as Anton Dubois. Is that your real name?"

"Yes." It wasn't true; Anton's papers were forged.

"I ask because this morning we inquired with the three Dubois families in the area and none of them admitted to knowing you."

"Not surprising if it was your Gestapo making the inquiry. But in fact, I arrived here less than a year ago, from the South." Anton was careful to mask his otherwise perfect English with a slight French accent.

"Then clearly you are not the leader of this little Resistance cell. Perhaps it is Michel Depierre, or maybe the man that was shot?" Anton did not respond. "From whom did your little group receive its orders?"

"We knew the man only as *Le Furet*—The Ferret. I never met him."

"You are from Corsica, according to your papers. Tell me a little about your home town." The major was trying to catch Anton in a lie, but the young flyer could provide a plausible response to this question as his paternal grandparents had emigrated from the island of Corsica in the 1890s.

"I was born in Calvi—on the northwest side of the island." *Another lie.* "Two thousand citizens and probably much like most other small French coastal towns. What else can I tell you? Some say that Christopher Columbus was born in Calvi." Anton sounded convincing. Fortunately, Grandfather Devereux had made a point of teaching young Anton about his roots.

"Let me tell you, Herr Dubois, what would have been your fate—as well as that of your friend—had you been caught in your act of sabotage just one month ago. This interview would have been decidedly more intense. You would have disclosed your real name as well as providing details concerning the activities of your Resistance cell. The guards at the door would apply their physical powers of persuasion in the event that you seemed reluctant to provide truthful answers. At the conclusion of the interview, you and your friend would be taken out into the courtyard, tied to the posts there, and shot." The Major paused briefly, searching Anton's face for any reaction to his words. There was none and the Major continued, "It is with some regret that I must inform you that your life will be spared—at least temporarily—in order that you might serve *der Führer.*"

Now Anton's curiosity was piqued. "Sounds interesting. Tell me more," he said.

"A recent directive from Berlin commutes the usual death sentence for captured spies and saboteurs—except for those determined to be responsible for the murder of our soldiers or officials. There is a critical shortage of manpower in some essential war industries and your services are required. In a few days, you and Herr Depierre will be transported to a work camp near Nordhausen."

"Very good," said Anton, "I'm told that Nordhausen can be enchanting this time of year." The Major started to respond to Anton's smart remark but stopped short of speaking. Finally he ordered the guards to take the prisoner back to his cell.

CHAPTER EIGHT

Mittelbau Dora
Concentration Camp
April 1944

THE TRANSPORT TRAIN CARRYING Michel Depierre and Anton Devereux and one hundred-fifty other conscripted French workers had arrived at Mittelbau Dora near Nordhausen in central Germany two months earlier. Since their arrival the population of the camp had swelled from less than one thousand to more than fifteen thousand with more new laborers arriving every week from German-occupied territories throughout Europe.

The Mittelwerk Production Facility was located deep underground inside an abandoned gypsum mine. It initially served as a fuel and oil depot for the army but became a preferred site for war production as more and more above-ground factories were destroyed by Allied bombing. By the end of the war, Mittelwerk production lines would be established for aircraft engines as well as the V-1 flying bomb and V-2 ballistic missile.

Michel and Anton were assigned work preparing the V-2 assembly area for full-scale rocket production.

Both working and living conditions at the labor camp were deplorable. Before the construction of barracks could be completed the prisoners lived in the tunnels where they worked. Death was commonplace due to disease, malnutrition and brutality from the guards, and trucks carrying the corpses of the deceased made frequent trips to the Buchenwald concentration camp for cremation.

"I'M NOT SURE how much longer I can do this," Anton whispered to his friend.

"What do you mean?" Michel asked.

"I mean I'm tired, weak, hungry. We both are; no—we all are—all of the laborers in this camp. The Nazis are working us to death." Anton had been struggling to move a large wooden crate containing gyroscope assemblies. The V-2 design called for two gyroscopes, one each mounted vertically and horizontally, to provide for stabilization during flight. Anton was out of breath and sat on the crate to rest.

"What's the alternative?" said Michel. "You saw what happened to the Polish kid." Henryk Milczarek was nineteen years old and had arrived at Mittelbau Dora a month after Michel and Anton. Two days earlier he fell from some high scaffolding and lay on his back in severe pain. When a Nazi guard ordered him back to work, Henryk could not—or would not—get up. The guard took out his side arm and shot the boy in the head.

"You can't give up," Michel continued. "This place exists because the Americans and the British are bombing the shit out of German factories and cities. It won't be long—maybe just a few months before an Allied invasion landing in France or maybe Holland. Now, get up. I'll help you with the crate."

A guard had come near the two men before Anton could move. "*Was ist los? Zurück zur Arbeit!* Get back to work!"

"*Ja, Ja, Ja,*" muttered Anton as he slowly rose to his feet.

"Anton—don't antagonize the guard, please," said Michel.

AS SPRING TURNED TO SUMMER the pervasive sense of hopelessness among the prisoner population abated somewhat. It wasn't because the working hours were shortened—they weren't—and the food was certainly no better, but the exhausting construction effort preparing the Mittelwerk V-2 production line was now complete and the prisoners were reassigned to the far less strenuous task of actually building the rockets.

The completed hardware subassemblies were subjected to a rigorous inspection by German technicians who demanded the highest quality work from the laborers. A few workers dared to purposely miswire or otherwise sabotage random critical components in hope that the missiles assembled with those faulty parts would fail at launch or in flight. Several laborers were caught engaging in such subterfuge. In each case, the perpetrator was first subjected to a severe beating and then strangled to death by hanging him from a crane in the assembly area as a warning to the rest of the workforce.

The first truly good news to be received at the camp since its inception was brought by new conscripts from France during the second week of June. They reported that an Allied invasion force—including Free French units— had successfully landed on the beaches of Normandy. A secure beachhead had been established and troops were moving inland. The expectation was that Paris would be liberated within a few weeks.

"Did you hear the good news, Fritz?" Anton had engaged one of the guards—one with whom he had frequently exchanged teasing jests. This guard—Fritz was not his real name—had always been strict with the prisoners, but at least treated them with some consideration. The exchanges had the effect of reducing tension in the work area, although some of the other laborers feared that Anton's comments would be considered disrespectful. If so, the Nazi response could be harsh.

" 'Vat good news?" The guard spoke passable English.

"News that the Allies are coming. You know, the British, Americans, Canadians. Even the Free French. They've landed in France and Germany will be next."

"It is probably a lie, but if they have come, our Panzers 'vill drive them back into the sea. Just like *die Engländer* at Dunkirk."

"I wouldn't be so sure about that. Maybe you should try to get a transfer to the Eastern Front. I heard that the *Kommandant* is planning a visit to some of the eastern concentration camps, hoping to rescue the Jewish children."

The guard looked about to make sure no other Germans were within earshot, and then cautioned, "Be careful. Don't make jokes like that; someone may hear you."

IT WASN'T LONG after the start of full-scale factory production that the V-2 production managers realized that the long work days imposed on the prisoners—sometimes more than sixteen hours a day—was not sustainable and resulted in poor quality work. Extreme fatigue was often responsible for unintentional mistakes that required scrapping or reworking critical assemblies.

The managers settled on two shifts of twelve hours each with the production line operating seven days week. Upon completion of each shift, the workers were marched to the recently completed barracks outside the south entrance of the Mittelwerk facility—a prisoner barracks known as Mittelbau Dora. There they would be issued their main meal for the day and could sleep or socialize for an hour or two in small groups—always under the watchful supervision of the guards. Each worker was assigned a sleeping bunk that was shared with an individual from the opposite shift. The men were mustered outside for inspection one-half hour before their next work shift began and given a second smaller meal before being marched back inside Mittelwerk to the production line for another twelve-hour shift.

MICHEL AND ANTON SAT OUTSIDE at the rear of the wooden barracks building to which they had been assigned. It was one of 58 structures that housed the prisoners, the "detainees," as they were called by their German overseers. They had finished their meal of watery potato soup and stale black bread and sat with their backs against the outside wall of the building, taking in the warm sunlight. It had been a few days since the prisoner workers last switched between day and night shifts, a scheduled change that occurred every four weeks. Now working on the day shift that ended at 5 PM, it had been a month since their previous opportunity to be outside during daylight hours.

"What are you doing, Anton?" Michel asked his friend.

"Why? What do you mean?

"Why are you feeding these damn birds?

They are just pests." Their barracks building was at the southwestern edge of the camp, and a flock of pigeons had been roosting under the eaves of a half dozen buildings at the camp's perimeter. Since the shift change Anton had tried to coax some of the birds down to the ground by cooing at them and offering small bits of bread as an enticement. A few of the birds had overcome their fear and even taken crumbs from Anton's open palm.

"I raised pigeons when I was a kid. They relax me." Anton broke the last small crust of bread in half and tossed a piece to each of the two pigeons on the ground near his feet. The birds picked up the bread in their beaks and made the short flight to a nest on a beam overhead. "A few of the men have even given me some of their bread for the birds."

"Don't let the guards find out," Michel quipped, "or they will cut our food rations."

CHAPTER NINE

Mittelwerk Production
Facility, Near Nordhausen
April 1945

MILITARY PLANNERS ON BOTH SIDES understood that the War in Europe was coming to an end. After crossing the German frontier in October 1944, the Soviet Army was now making a final assault on Berlin. Artillery shelling began on April 20 and the City was completely encircled by the Soviets within a few days. In the West the Allies secured a vital bridge across the Rhine at Remagen on March 7 and were proceeding east, taking thousands of German troops as prisoners along the way.

Benito Mussolini was captured by Italian partisans on April 27 and executed and strung up in Milan the next day, together with his mistress. The Italian army and German forces in Italy surrendered on April 29.

With the Soviets only a few blocks from his underground bunker, Adolf Hitler and his mistress, Eva Braun, committed suicide hours after they wedded in a simple marriage ceremony. Their bodies were burned and buried in a shallow grave by Hitler's aides before Soviet troops reached the bunker.

Hitler had appointed Admiral Karl Dönitz as his successor. Within a few days, Dönitz would order all German U-boats to cease offensive operations and return to their home ports. Under orders from the Admiral, General Jodl would sign the document of unconditional surrender to the Western Allied forces at a ceremony in Reims on May 7. Field Marshall Keitel would sign a similar document with the Soviets in Berlin the next day.

Hitler had hoped that the revolutionary new weapons developed by his scientists and engineers would change the course of the War before it was too late. Some of the weapon systems were indeed revolutionary including the Messerschmitt Me262 jet-powered fighter. Although development of this first-of-its-kind jet aircraft began before the War, it did not become operational until mid-1944. The delay was due in large part to reliability problems associated with the high combustion chamber temperatures in the turbofan engines. Efforts aimed at identifying and implementing a suitable high-temperature metal alloy were only partially successful, and operational aircraft were subject to frequent engine replacement.

More than 1,400 Me262s were produced by war's end. While high speed—a hundred miles per hour faster than piston-engine powered fighters of the day—made it formidable in attacking British and American bombers, its introduction so late in the conflict could not turn the tide of the air war in Germany's favor.

Even more revolutionary was the V-2 ballistic missile. Production had begun at Mittelwerk in August 1944 with the first operational launches directed at Paris on September 6. Although the first two missiles failed, most subsequent missile firings were successful. V-2 attacks on London began on September 8, 1944.

Total V-2 production at Mittelwerk was nearly 4,600 units with the completed missiles delivered to launch sites in western France. Warheads and fuel—the alcohol-water mixture and liquid oxygen—were added just prior to launch. The Germans also developed a portable missile launching system for the V-2. The truck-mounted units came into widespread use after most of the fixed launch sites were overrun by the advancing Allies.

London and Antwerp were the most frequently targeted cities by V-2 missiles. Attacks on the Port of Antwerp were intended to disrupt the flow of war matériel and slow the Allied advance toward Germany. With the Allies making important advances in France, some elements of the German High Command believed that subjecting England to enough devastation from V-2 attacks might induce the Western Allies to agree to a separate peace treaty. Overall, the V-2 was responsible for some 7,000 Allied civilian and military deaths, but like the Me262 and other German "wonder weapons," it was clearly a case of "too little, too late."

"FRITZ JUST TOLD ME something interesting," Anton whispered to his friend. Anton had returned from a latrine break to where he and Michel had been assembling parts for the V-2 alcohol-water fuel pumps.

"Tell me that the War is over."

Anton ignored his friend's remark and looked about to make sure no one was listening. "Night shift production is being shut down. All night shift workers will be reassigned to facilities in the east—whatever that means. It starts today."

"What about us—the dayshift?"

"We'll be around here for a little while. They want us to complete and ship any rockets that are more than fifty-percent complete. They just don't need two shifts to do the work."

"That shouldn't take longer than two or three weeks," offered Michel. "Then . . . what?"

"He didn't say, but I don't think they would be doing this unless the Brits or Americans were closing in."

Fritz passed on some more information the next day. Anton learned that the night shift workers were divided into three groups. The first group, workers with the highest technical skills, were marched to the railroad yards and herded into boxcars for the trip east. Fritz didn't know the destination. German night shift supervisors were also on that train, presumably with better accommodations. The lowest-skilled workers, consisting primarily of less-educated Poles, Russians and Ukrainians, were sent to a temporary camp near the railroad yards, to await transport to Buchenwald. The sickest workers in the night shift—about two hundred in total—made up the third group. They were taken to Boelcke Kaserne, a former military barracks near the town of Nordhausen. Sick workers from the other Mittelwerk production projects were sent to the same camp.

Wernher von Braun and his team of scientists and engineers were relocated to Oberammergau in the Bavarian Alps. The area was under SS control and secret orders had been issued to "liquidate" the entire team rather than allow it to fall into Allied hands. Von Braun either knew or suspected that such an order had been issued and successfully convinced SS General Hans Kammler that the team members should be dispersed to neighboring villages. In the event of a bombing raid, it was argued, the entire team would not be lost. In order to survive the War, von Braun wanted above all to surrender his team to the advancing Americans, avoiding the Russians. Before leaving Mittelwerk he made arrangements for V-2 design blueprints to be hidden in an abandoned mineshaft near Nordhausen.

"YOU HEARD THE BOMBS LAST NIGHT?"

"Of course. They kept me awake." Anton and Michel were resting behind their barracks building after completing their shift. The two had recently been assigned to separate assembly areas and this was their first opportunity of the day to talk. "Fritz told me that Boelcke Kaserne was flattened in the raid, killing nearly everyone in the camp."

"No. Really? It is terrible thing," said Michel, "that British or American bombers would kill our people."

"I'm sure they believed only German soldiers were in the camp."

"It worries me. If the bombing continues, they will likely kill all of us. Maybe we should try to escape," offered Michel.

"You're suggesting we somehow get through the barbed wire, avoiding the search lights and machine guns in the guard towers? And then we simply walk to the American lines, wearing our best striped pajamas?"

"Better to try to escape than to be blown up in our sleep."

"Maybe instead we can get word to the Americans," said Anton, "that there are so many prisoners here."

"Certainly. I'm sure if you asked, you could call the American Army from the telephone in the Commandant's office," Michel quipped.

"No. Not the telephone. I'm thinking of the bird—the pigeon that flew in yesterday. I thought he'd fly off, but he's still here." Anton pointed up at the roof to where the blue-gray pigeon was resting with its head partially buried under one wing, appearing content to absorb a little heat from the last rays of the setting sun. When first offering the pigeon some scraps of bread the day before, Anton noticed the small leather message capsule that was strapped to one leg. He knew that pigeons were used extensively for communication during World War I, but was surprised that they were still being used to carry messages.

Some feathers were missing from one wing tip—evidence of an injury—and the bird seemed comfortable to be held in Anton's hands. Anton and Michel didn't know why the pigeon had come to Mittelbau Dora instead of its "home" location—probably some command post behind the American lines. Perhaps it was due to the wing injury.

The message inside the capsule was coded using English words and numbers. Most likely it had been prepared by an Allied reconnaissance patrol in order to report on enemy troop positions and strength. Understanding that the message might contain vital information, Anton returned the message to the capsule, intent on sending the bird on its way. Now, a day later with the pigeon still in the camp, Anton held out a piece of bread for the bird, contemplating what he should write as an addendum to the coded message.

CHAPTER TEN

Cedarpines Park, California
Christmas Day 1964

"I'VE HEARD ONLY BITS and pieces of the story, Grandma." Jason and Pamela were in the kitchen having breakfast. A cold front had moved into the San Bernardino Mountains overnight, and they watched the light snow falling outside. "When Robert and I were on speaking terms, it was brought up from time to time. He didn't believe a word of it—thought that there was maybe something about Dad that you and Granddad were trying to cover up."

"You mean like the story that your father was convicted of passing Royal Air Force secrets to the Nazis and spent five years after the war in a Federal prison?" offered Pamela.

"That was one of the rumors. Another one that Robert heard was that my Dad flew his Spitfire across the border into Switzerland, met a woman there and raised a second family."

"I guess that when people find it hard to believe what you're telling them, they tend to speculate about other possibilities. That's how rumors start. And that's why your grandfather and I stopped talking about it."

"Well, Grandma, I'd like to hear the whole story from you—from the beginning."

"It's been fifteen years, but I still remember like it happened yesterday." Pamela paused briefly, collecting her thoughts before continuing, "It was September 1950. Your grandfather and I were sitting at this very table. We had finished our breakfast and were watching the birds come and go near the aviary. We called it *the aviary* just to give it a name, but no birds were ever confined there; they could always come and go as they pleased. Anyway, after a few minutes your grandfather got up from the table and went to the window. Something on the deck outside had grabbed his attention." . . .

"PAMELA, COME HERE, would you? There's something strange about that pigeon."

"Which one?"

"That one, there," Bertrand pointed, "on top of the aviary. There is something wrong with his leg. Looks like it's wrapped in a splint."

Bertrand stepped out on the deck and slowly approached the pigeon. The bird seemed quite tame and made no attempt to take flight, even as Bertrand extended his hands and gently grasped the bird. Now Bertrand could see that the pigeon's leg was not injured, but attached to it was a small leather capsule.

Bertrand twisted the top off the capsule and pulled out a short length of rolled up paper, about the size and length of a half smoked cigarette. He held it between his thumb and index finger, staring at it as he shuffled back into the kitchen and returned to his place at the table.

"What is it?" Pamela asked.

"Some kind of message, I think." Bertrand had unrolled it and then unfolded the thin buff-colored paper—now a piece about three inches square that had been folded in half before being rolled up. He had to hold down the corners of the paper in order to keep it flat.

"What does it say?"

"It doesn't make sense; just some words, letters and numbers." He read it aloud, "FALL FORCE 100 X N WITH 6 HEAVY NOW 4 K EAST 3 K NORTH POINT BRAVO."

"There is something written on the other side," said Pamela. She watched as Bertrand turned the paper over. After several seconds, she couldn't help but notice the color draining from her husband's face. Without saying a word, he slid the paper toward his wife. She raised her reading glasses from the chain around her neck and read the message to herself:

ON 2 APRIL BOMBING OF FORMER GERMAN BARRACKS NEAR NORDHAUSEN KILLED MORE THAN 1,500 FORCED LABORERS—FRENCH,

POLISH AND RUSSIAN—HOUSED THERE. MANY MORE PRISONERS ARE IN LABOR CAMPS SOUTH AND EAST OF BOMBED CAMP. PLEASE SEND GROUND FORCES TO LIBERATE CAMPS, NOT BOMBS.

There was a signature and date that read:

ANTON DEVEREUX – RAF 4-APR-1945

"Oh my," exclaimed Pamela, "how could this be? This is Anton's signature; I'm sure of it." She removed her glasses and buried her face in her hands.

"I don't know," said Bertrand, "but I'm going to call Charlie Prince. Maybe he can tell us what this means."

CHARLIE PRINCE WORKED in the Office of the Assistant Secretary of War until his retirement in December 1945. He was highly regarded for his expertise in logistics planning and had spent much of the last year of his career developing plans for the invasion of Japan—plans that were not needed after the Japanese surrendered in August 1945.

Charlie was a California native and returned to the State after his retirement. He and his wife, Julia, had purchased a small farm house less than one-half mile from the home of Pamela and Bertrand Devereux. Pamela and Julia met at the local Women's Club where they had both volunteered for some community service projects. The two couples began to spend time together, often playing contract bridge in the afternoons.

Upon first hearing about Anton Devereux and learning that Pamela and Bertrand still knew nothing about the fate of their son after seven long years, Charlie Prince asked a few of his former War Department contacts to look into the matter. They were able to obtain a copy of Anton's service record with the RAF, but there was no information about the young flyer after the day his Spitfire was shot down over France.

Pamela and Bertrand held no expectation that Charlie's efforts would bring their son home alive, but it was a crushing disappointment that no new information could be learned. Now, nearly four years later, the Devereuxs had reason for renewed hope concerning their son thanks to the newly received message—a message delivered to their home by a pigeon. Bertrand took the message to Charlie Prince.

"I believe some sick individual is trying to play a cruel joke here," Charlie said after examining the scrap of paper that Bertrand showed him. "I'm sorry, but I don't believe a pigeon is able to fly from France to California."

"You're right about that," said Bertrand, "I raised pigeons years ago and remember reading somewhere that the record flying distance for a homing pigeon was something like one thousand miles." He paused before continuing, "But that *is* my son's signature. He wrote that message five years ago in order to save his own life and the lives of hundreds—maybe thousands—of poor bastard prisoners of the Nazis. I'm sure of it."

"I want to speak with some other people I know in Washington," said Charlie. "Maybe they can verify that bombing raid on—" Charlie looked down at the message, "—on that camp near Nordhausen and what may have happened afterword. Give me a few days."

CHAPTER ELEVEN

Europe
April 1945

THE WARNING MESSAGE that Anton Devereux composed never reached the Allied base camp—the "home" destination for his feathered messenger.

The Bomb Damage Assessment Team analysis of British Bomber Command's April 2 raid near Nordhausen concluded that the mission was an unqualified success. In particular, reconnaissance photos of Boelcke Kaserne revealed that the German barracks and nearby fuel and ammunition depots were obliterated in the raid. Plans were immediately drawn up to extend the target area for additional saturation bombing to include the Mittelwerk facility itself and the railhead where completed V-weapons were being loaded on flat cars for shipment to launch sites.

British Lancaster bombers dropped 600 tons of bombs on each of three successive nights beginning April 8. The Mittelwerk production facilities, buried deep underground, were left largely undamaged by the bombing, but anything above ground was reduced to rubble. Tragically, the bomber crews were oblivious to the death and destruction they unknowingly rained down on helpless French, Polish and Russian detainees in the labor concentration camps outside Mittelwerk.

The series of raids had other unintended consequences that would prove to be historically significant. Photo reconnaissance conducted after the bombing led planners to conclude that the area had been neutralized, and original plans for the advance into the Nordhausen region by American forces were cancelled. Instead, the American Third Armored Division, an element of the U.S. First Army, was ordered to skirt north of Nordhausen and commence a spearhead drive toward Berlin. At the same time, General Patton's Third Army was approaching Berlin from a staging area near Hanover. The two U.S. battle groups reached the outskirts of the City only to find that the Soviets had arrived there a few days earlier and had Berlin encircled.

The Soviets recognized an opportunity after the bombing and moved quickly to fill the vacuum in the Nordhausen region. They entered Mittelwerk nearly unopposed. The remaining German forces were quickly neutralized, and the Russian Army captured the production facilities and dozens of completed and nearly-complete missiles virtually intact.

The Russians now stood between Wernher von Braun's team and the American lines. The team's only hope to avoid being captured by the Russians was to head south into Switzerland. But the large caravan of trucks and cars was interdicted by the Red Army near Innsbruck, and von Braun's entire science and engineering team was escorted back to Mittelwerk and interred there. The team members were put to work, dismantling the V-2 production facilities. Within a few weeks, the entire team, together with all tools, drawings and dozens of fully and partially assembled V-2 rockets would be sent east into Russia.

The Allied heads of state—Franklin Roosevelt, Winston Churchill and Joseph Stalin—had previously met at Yalta in February 1945 to establish plans for post-war management of Germany. It was agreed that Germany would be divided up into four sectors: one each American, British and French and a zone controlled by the Soviets in the East. Because the Soviets had made the greatest gains in their westward push, Berlin—the German capital—would be deep inside the Soviet sector and provisions were made to divide the city itself in four zones of occupation.

When hostilities ended in early May 1945, General Patton was ordered to give up his positions at the outskirts of Berlin and move his forces back inside the agreed upon border of the American Zone. He refused and was quoted as saying, "Hundreds of American boys died securing this territory and I am not turning it over to some goddamn Communist sons-of-bitches." The Soviet response was immediate. General Zhukov ordered ten tank divisions from positions east of Berlin to head west and prepare to engage the Americans.

After some emergency diplomatic initiatives, Patton was relieved of his command by President Truman and ordered home. The U.S. Third Army moved back to the American Zone, defusing the crisis and the very real possibility of military conflict between the two Allied powers.

Back home, Patton was regarded as a hero for standing up against the Soviets. Three years later he would challenge Harry Truman in the Presidential Election of 1948, running as an Independent, facing both Truman and Thomas Dewey, the Republican challenger. The Berlin Crisis of 1945 was generally regarded as the beginning of the Cold War between the Soviet Union and the United States.

The twin Soviet successes of capturing the V-2 production facilities at Mittelwerk intact as well as Wernher von Braun's team of missile scientists and engineers would soon propel the Soviet Union to the position of undisputed world leader in missile and space technology.

A development complex was established in Central Siberia known as the Krasnoyarsk Aerospace Technology Center. Multiple successful launches of captured V-2 rockets, now designated as the Russian R-1, were conducted beginning in December 1945 and a production line for new R-1 copies of the V-2 was operational by March 1946.

With the help of von Braun's team, the missile range was increased from 320 to 400 kilometers. Later that year, a two-stage ballistic missile was test-fired into the Northern Pacific Ocean from Krasnoyarsk, a distance of 5,500 kilometers. This missile design was based on the German A10 rocket, still unfinished at the end of the War but intended to strike New York and other eastern U.S. coastal cities from launch sites on the Atlantic coast of France.

Meanwhile, the U.S. missile development program was foundering. Not more than fifty German rocket technicians could be identified in the American Zone and taken to White Sands Proving Ground in New Mexico. Contrast this with the more than 500 German scientists and engineers that were sent to the Soviet Union. Fewer than a dozen operational V-2 rockets fell into British and American hands, and most early launch attempts ended in failure.

The consensus in Washington was that the American missile program suffered from a lack of direction. The Army had hoped that Robert Goddard might be selected to head up missile development and testing, but Goddard had serious health problems and died in August 1945.

Although remaining well behind the Soviets in missile development, America was the lone world nuclear power for multiple years following the end of World War Two. The Soviet occupation zone in Germany included several prestigious research facilities, including the Kaiser Wilhelm Institute for Physics in Berlin and its cadre of top scientists that included Werner Heisenberg and Walther Bothe.

The Soviets hoped to build on German atomic weapons development that began in 1939, but during the occupation it was learned that the German program had been severely scaled back as early as 1942. The Germans concluded early on that no weapon could be developed in time to affect the outcome of the war.

The Soviets were determined to hide their lack of progress on atomic bomb development from the Western powers, but the sensitive information was leaked to a British agent by a German physicist reassigned from Mittelwerk to the Berlin Institute. The same agent also reported that the Soviets had recently received some vital test data concerning uranium isotope separation from spies working in the American Manhattan Project. The Americans were shocked to learn that security at Los Alamos had been breached, but they were quick to respond. The spies were arrested before any more significant atomic secrets were compromised.

Unable to benefit from the limited state of German atomic development and the poor results from their atomic espionage efforts, it was generally believed that an operational

Soviet weapon was years—perhaps a decade or more—away. Although the Soviets had not yet joined the U.S. in the "nuclear club," American concerns were still focused on the Soviet's clear superiority in missile technology. Eventually, it was feared, an atomic warhead would be mated to a long range Soviet ballistic missile.

As Election Day in November 1948 approached, political pundits expressed divided opinions concerning the impact of General Patton's candidacy on election results. Extensive polling suggested that Patton could not win the election, but by receiving an expected fifteen percent of the popular vote he was viewed as a serious "spoiler."

The question was who would lose the most votes to Patton? It was not known whether the majority of his supporters were disaffected Democrats, who would have otherwise cast their vote for the incumbent Truman, or unhappy Republicans who clearly would support the challenger, Thomas Dewey.

The very last pre-election polls predicted Truman would win with a paper-thin margin, and the headline of an early morning edition of the *Chicago Daily Tribune* on November 3, 1948, prematurely proclaimed "TRUMAN DEFEATS DEWEY." But it wasn't to be. Thomas Dewey became the 34th President of the United States.

Dewey's win was attributed to his record as a tough Federal prosecutor and strong anti-Communist commitment that played well with most Americans who viewed expansion of Communism abroad as a serious threat. Many voters simply felt it was time for a change as a Democrat had occupied the White House continuously since 1932.

It was only a few months after Inauguration Day before the new Administration would be tested. In China, Mao and his Red Army were defeating Chiang-Kai-Shek's Nationalists in nearly every engagement. During World War II and the Japanese occupation, differences between the two factions had been set aside in order to defeat the hated Japanese invaders. The conflict between the Communists and Nationalists resumed at the close of the War and in recent years had escalated significantly.

"I WISH I COULD bring you some encouraging news about your son," said Charlie Prince. Charlie had come to the home of Bertrand and Pamela Devereux just three days after their previous meeting. "There were many Allied units present west of Nordhausen on April 4, the date on Anton's message. It seems that either no one in authority received or read it, or they chose to ignore the information. British bombers pounded the area a few days later, and it is likely that few of the camp detainees survived. I'm sorry."

Pamela cried softly while Bertrand raised one hand to his forehead and looked down at the floor, dejected. "I understand," he said.

"It was a tragic situation," Charlie continued. "The bombs killed hundreds—maybe thousands—of helpless prisoners and resulted in such widespread devastation that our Army units believed that occupying the area would have little military value. The Army left the region and set their sights on Berlin, unaware that an invaluable cache of the most advanced weapons in the Nazi arsenal was left intact, safely hidden deep underground and free for the taking.

"The Russians moved in and took everything of value including hundreds of top German scientists. Among them was a man by the name of von Braun—a real scientific genius—it turns out. It's why our country is so far behind the Russians in missile and jet aircraft development." Charlie paused briefly and then quickly added, "But don't tell anyone I told you that."

CHAPTER TWELVE

Cedarpines Park, California
Christmas Day 1964

"SO THIS CHARLIE—" said Jason Devereux, sitting across from his grandmother at the kitchen table.

"Yes, Charlie Prince," added Pamela.

"He believed that Dad was killed in the British bombing raid, correct?"

"Yes, Jason." Now Pamela leaned forward in her chair with her face directly in front of her grandson's and spoke slowly, carefully enunciating each word. "I believe it also; I believe your father *was* killed in that raid."

"I don't understand."

"That pigeon showed up again after Charlie Prince left our house that morning. In fact, that bird returned for a few minutes every day since the day it first arrived carrying your father's message. By then, your grandfather had even named the bird—Bradley, he called him. But this time it was perched on the window sill and began pecking at the glass. When your grandfather walked out to the deck for a closer look, Bradley flew down to the deck railing out there."

Pamela pointed to the stairway outside leading down from the deck to the backyard. "And when your grandfather moved toward the stairs, Bradley flew down to the ground below the deck. Each time he approached that bird it would fly to a point a few yards away from him. It was as if that pigeon was purposely leading your grandfather away from the house and toward the tree line. . . ."

PAMELA DEVEREUX WATCHED from the kitchen window until Bertrand and the pigeon named Bradley disappeared from view. The bird led Bertrand deep into the woods, alighting on the branch of one tree after another; moving on as Bertrand came closer, always staying a few yards ahead of the man.

What am I doing here, following this silly bird? Bertrand asked himself. After fifteen minutes he considered turning back and returning to the house, but now he was curious and decided to press on.

When he emerged from the forest ten minutes later, Bertrand found himself on a narrow gravel road that connected up ahead with a paved highway at a T-intersection. A painted wooden sign stood at the intersection pointing to the right that read "VASPERVILLER 2 KM" and one immediately below it pointing left: "SAINT-QUIRIN 1 KM."

Now he was confused. Bertrand guessed he was less than two miles west of his home and knew of no other close towns in that direction. Nor was he familiar with the names on the signs.

Bradley made a couple of circular passes above Bertrand's head and then flew off toward the town on the left. Bertrand could see some buildings in the distance and decided to follow.

As he came closer to the town he passed a sign on the shoulder of the road that read *Bienvenue au Village de Saint-Quirin:* "Welcome to the Village of Saint-Quirin." Bertrand didn't understand why the welcome sign was in French, but at least he understood it as Bertrand was fluent in the language.

Nothing he had seen since leaving the forest made any sense. The village itself was picturesque with shops lining both sides of the highway and oddly dressed people going about their daily business. The entire town was only four or five streets wide and ran for maybe a quarter of a mile along the highway.

The wisps of conversation he heard as he passed couples in the street were all in French—one man asking his wife if they needed to buy bread for their dinner; another complained that his shoes did not fit—they were too small.

It had been an hour since Bertrand left his home and he was tired. The coffee shop at the corner seemed like a good place to rest for a few minutes. A waiter approached as he sat at one of the outdoor tables.

"Un café?" the waiter asked.

Sure—why not, thought Bertrand. *"Oui."*

A well-dressed elderly man—brown suit and beret, no tie—sat alone at a table nearby reading the front page of a newspaper. When he raised the paper, holding it up with both hands in order to turn to an inside page, Bertrand couldn't help but notice the front page headlines now just a few feet away from him:

ARMÉE ROUGE APPROCHAIT BERLINE

What the hell? thought Bertrand, *the Red Army? Near Berlin?* He and Pamela hadn't seen any television news that morning because of Charlie Prince's visit. Whatever was going on must have started overnight, but why would the Russian Army go back into East Germany now? They had left months earlier after putting their Communist shills in charge of the country. *Maybe it was a revolt*, thought Bertrand.

"Monsieur?" Bertrand's attention was focused on the newspaper headlines and he hadn't noticed the waiter place the demitasse of coffee on the table in front of him.

"I'm sorry."

"Trente francs, s'il vous plait."

"Yes, I'm sorry," Bertrand repeated as he fumbled for his wallet. Not knowing the exchange rate, he pulled out three one dollar bills and placed them on the table. The waiter picked up one of the bills and muttered something about returning with his change; then approached the well-dressed Frenchman who had called him over to settle his bill.

The Frenchman stood and repositioned his beret, then turned toward Bertrand and offered his newspaper.

Merci, "Thank you," said Bertrand. The Frenchman nodded and walked off. Bertrand began to quickly scan the headline article of the Paris newspaper, *Paris-Presse*. When he read the description of the artillery bombardment at the outskirts of Berlin, Bertrand realized that something was amiss. He stopped reading momentarily to look at the masthead of the paper that showed the publication date, April 6, 1945. Now it was beginning to make some sense: the article was an account of events that had occurred more than five years ago.

The waiter returned to the table and left a few copper coins—seventy-five French francs in all—as change from the dollar. Bertrand looked about, unconsciously stroking the coins with his fingers for a minute or more before speaking aloud, to no one in particular, "I have no idea why or how, but this is France and the year is 1945. Not California in 1950."

CHAPTER THIRTEEN

Cedarpines Park, California
Christmas Day 1964

"YOU'VE TOLD ME that Grandfather Bertrand followed that pigeon—Bradley, was it?"

"Yes, he named the bird Bradley. I don't know why," said Pamela.

"He followed the bird into the forest, and when he came out on the other side, it was five years earlier and he was thousands of miles from here, in France. Is that right?"

"Yes. Correct."

"You know I love you very much, Grandma, but if that bird had been a rooster and there was a herd of cattle nearby, I'd ask you what kind of cock-and-bull story you were trying to tell me."

Pamela Devereux laughed at her grandson's remark. "I love you, too, Jason," she said, "and that's why I'm telling you all this. You should know the true story of how your grandfather saved your father's life."

"OK, but you haven't said anything about my father yet. What happened next?"

"My Bertrand asked the waiter at the coffee shop where there might be some American military units nearby. He was told there was an Army regional supply post in the next town—*Vasperviller,* it was called—just two miles away.

"Your grandfather was able to hitch a ride with a farmer in his donkey cart. Before meeting with the Post Commander, he decided it would be best not to mention that only hours earlier he had been several thousand miles away and five years in the future...."

BERTRAND DEVEREUX HAD TO WAIT for an hour before being ushered in to see Colonel Jacobsen, the Post Commander.

"You're an American, Mr. Devereux?" the Colonel asked. "How is it that you were able to come to France at this time? And why? In case you haven't noticed, there's still a war going on here."

"I'm from California and getting here wasn't very difficult. I flew to Madrid and crossed the border on foot a few weeks ago. I'm trying to locate some missing relatives." Bertrand continued, comfortable with the white lie he was telling the Colonel. "There are several cousins and uncles we should have heard from by now—since the liberation—but we've heard nothing from them. But I'm here today because of my son, Anton. He flew for the RAF and was shot down nearly two years ago. We believe he may have been rescued by some members of the French Resistance. I hoped to find him, or at least learn what may have happened to him. But yesterday I was given this message." Bertrand placed the message on Colonel Jacobsen's desk.

"This is a coded message," said the Colonel, "probably sent by pigeon from an Army recon unit near the front. What could this have to do with your son? "

"Turn the paper over, Colonel." Jacobsen read Anton's message as Bertrand continued. "I believe my son is alive—held in that concentration camp—probably with hundreds of other prisoners."

Colonel Jacobsen clasped his hands together, resting them on the message in front of him. "What would you have me do with this, Mister Devereux? It's a hundred and fifty miles to Nordhausen."

"Send someone to save my son—and the others. There must be some Army units near the camp. And get someone to stop the bombing. It's killing many innocent prisoners."

The Colonel considered Bertrand's request for several seconds before replying, "I know some people that may be able to help. If they can verify the details in your son's message, they may be willing to send in a team to liberate the camp."

"Thank you, Colonel." The men stood together and shook hands. Colonel Jacobsen picked up his telephone handset as Bertrand left the office.

Bertrand didn't know what he should do now or even where to go. He headed back toward Saint-Quirin. When he reached the intersection he found Bradley the pigeon perched on one of the direction signs.

CHAPTER FOURTEEN

Cedarpines Park, California
September 1950

BERTRAND DEVEREUX FOLLOWED the pigeon back through the forest, unsure of where the bird was leading him until the back of his house came into view with his wife, Pamela, standing on the deck.

"I was ready to call the sheriff," she said. "You've been gone for an hour. I was worried."

"Is there any coffee? I need a cup," Bertrand announced.

Pamela sat with her husband at the kitchen table for the next half hour as Bertrand told her the details of his sojourn to the French countryside circa 1945. She had no reason to believe her husband would fabricate such a story, but she was concerned about his mental state. To her, he seemed overly excited—almost agitated.

"Are you sure you're feeling all right?" she asked. "Maybe you should lie down for a few minutes."

"Not now, Pamela. I need to call Charlie Prince and find out what all this means."

"Bertrand! Listen to me. You can't call Charlie."

"What do you mean?" he asked, "Why not?"

"Because Charlie Prince died a month ago. Don't you remember? We went to his memorial service."

It was clear to Bertrand that he and Pamela had met with Charlie Prince that very morning—a fact that simply did not comport with Pamela's claim that Charlie died a month earlier. At their meeting Charlie was quite alive, disclosing to them the bombing of the concentration camps around Nordhausen. Bertrand refused to believe what his wife was telling him until she showed him a copy of Charlie's memorial service program.

"You're sure I was there?" he asked.

"I'm going to make an appointment for you to see Doctor Jensen," she said.

DURING THE NEXT FEW DAYS Bertrand would learn that much of what he believed to be historical fact was somehow no longer true or altered in a significant way. Periodicals at the local library revealed that his understanding of the state of the world in 1950 had been all wrong.

He read an article about the Presidential Election of 1948 that made no mention of General George Patton as a third party candidate. He found a biography of Patton on the book shelves and learned why: General Patton suffered a severe head injury in a car accident in Germany on December 9, 1945, and died in the hospital several days later.

Bertrand was surprised to learn that more than a year earlier, in August 1949, the Soviet Union shocked the world by exploding its first atomic bomb in what is now Kazakhstan. The successful first test came early thanks to atomic secrets disclosed to the Soviets by spies—notably Klaus Fuchs and David Greenglass—within the Manhattan Project at Los Alamos.

Fuchs was a British theoretical physicist of German descent with access to critical design details about the bomb while David Greenglass was a machinist who provided information about atomic lab experiments. Bertrand read that Greenglass was the brother of Ethel Rosenberg who together with her husband Julius had recently been indicted by a Federal Grand Jury for conspiracy to commit espionage by passing American bomb secrets to Soviet operatives.

Bertrand found dozens of articles about Soviet atomic bomb testing and the arrest of alleged Soviet agents caught spying in America, but there seemed to be little in the news about the advances in Soviet missile technology. Comparing weapons programs before and after Bertrand's quick trip to France across space and time, it was as if the Russians traded their lead in missile technology for membership in the nuclear club. It began to make more sense to Bertrand when he learned that that an important German scientist with the name Wernher von Braun and hundreds of former German missile experts had been brought to the United States—and not to the Soviet Union—at the end of the war.

As the weeks passed, Bertrand finally accepted the notion that it was his strange trip back to wartime France and the meeting with Colonel Jacobsen that set into motion a series of events that effectively rewrote the last five years of history.

CHAPTER FIFTEEN

"YOU UNDERSTAND, WERNHER, that since your recent successful V-2 tests at Peenemünde that *der Fuehrer* himself has expressed renewed interest and support for your work." Heinrich Himmler had summoned the missile expert to Gestapo headquarters to discuss the future of the project.

"Thank you, *Herr Reichsführer*," replied von Braun.

"But there are concerns. We believe that the ultimate success of the project may be in jeopardy if it remains under Army management."

"How so, *Herr Reichsführer*?"

"It is largely a matter of resources. The *Wehrmacht* is preoccupied with efforts to blunt the Soviet counter-offensive. And as you may know, there is a concern that the British and Americans may launch an invasion on the coast of France sometime this year. Vast Army labor and material resources have already been redirected toward building up coastal defenses.

Despite your successes, the Army is likely to abandon your work out of necessity. In contrast, here within the SS we have few conflicting preoccupations. Under our direction and support, your work can safely continue unimpeded."

"We have experienced some project setbacks, but none that I could attribute to my Army managers. Generals Zanssen and Dormberger have been most supportive in the past and have promised their continuing future support. If not for the disruption caused by the British bombing raid on Peenemünde and subsequent relocation to Nordhausen, I believe the V-2 would already be fully operational."

"Think it over, Wernher. I believe that a transfer to the SS would invigorate your project and also be in your personal best interest."

IT IS NOT KNOWN WHY Wernher von Braun turned down the proposal presented to him by Heinrich Himmler, but several days later he was arrested by Gestapo agents and imprisoned. There were charges that he held little personal interest in developing the V-2 as a military weapon, but instead saw it as an important step toward the exploration of space. He was also suspected of planning an escape to England by airplane, taking missile secrets to the enemy.

None of the charges were proven, and after two weeks of imprisonment General Dormberger made a direct appeal to Adolf

Hitler, insisting on von Braun's release. The General argued that "without von Braun, there would be no V-2." Hitler ordered an immediate release of Wernher von Braun from custody.

CHAPTER SIXTEEN

Berlin, Germany
December 1938

RADIOCHEMISTRY, THE STUDY of the chemical properties of radioactive materials, was an important area of research by physical scientists in the years following Marie Curie's discovery of radium and polonium in 1898. When two German radiochemists, Otto Hahn and Fritz Strassmann, were studying the effects of neutron bombardment on uranium in 1938, they made an unexpected discovery: many of the uranium atoms in their target sample disappeared—replaced, in fact, by one atom each of two lighter weight elements plus a few extra neutrons. But the reaction carried with it an unusual result in that the components into which the uranium atoms were split weighed somewhat less than the original uranium atoms. The difference was correctly attributed to the conversion of mass into energy.

Lise Meitner, a former Jewish colleague of Hahn who had escaped from Nazi Germany to

Sweden, later determined that the amount of energy released was consistent with Albert Einstein's famous mass-to-energy conversion equation, $E = mc^2$.

Just as significant was the realization that the extra neutron byproducts of the reaction could cause more uranium atoms to split, with more release of energy and more neutrons. Under the right conditions, a self-sustaining nuclear chain reaction could occur, releasing explosive quantities of energy in the form of light and heat.

The military implications of this discovery were obvious. Splitting of the atoms in a few kilograms of fissionable uranium could release enough energy to destroy an entire city. With the coming war in Europe only months away, the formerly free exchange of scientific data among researchers throughout the world came to an abrupt end. In America, there was a growing fear that Nazi scientists might soon be able to harness the power of the atom for the express purpose of creating terrible weapons of destruction.

Several European scientists left their home countries earlier in the 1930s to escape Nazi oppression. Among them were two Hungarians, Leo Szilard and Edward Teller, who believed that the threat of a nuclear-armed Nazi Germany must be brought to the attention of authorities at the highest level of the U.S. Government.

With the help of Szilard, the highly respected American scientist, Albert Einstein, drafted a letter to President Franklin Roosevelt alerting him to the findings of recent nuclear research and the potential weapons of mass destruction that might be added to Nazi arsenals. The August 1939 letter stated in part:

. . . THAT THE ELEMENT URANIUM MAY BE TURNED INTO A NEW AND IMPORTANT SOURCE OF ENERGY IN THE IMMEDIATE FUTURE. CERTAIN ASPECTS OF THE SITUATION WHICH HAS ARISEN SEEM TO CALL FOR WATCHFULNESS AND, IF NECESSARY, QUICK ACTION ON THE PART OF THE ADMINISTRATION.

The letter went on to state that

. . . IT MAY BECOME POSSIBLE TO SET UP A NUCLEAR CHAIN REACTION IN A LARGE MASS OF URANIUM, BY WHICH VAST AMOUNTS OF POWER AND LARGE QUANTITIES OF NEW RADIUM-LIKE ELEMENTS WOULD BE GENERATED. NOW IT APPEARS THAT THIS COULD BE ACHIEVED IN THE IMMEDIATE FUTURE.

THIS NEW PHENOMENOM WOULD ALSO LEAD TO THE CONSTRUCTION OF BOMBS . . . .

IN VIEW OF THIS SITUATION YOU MAY THINK IT DESIRABLE TO HAVE SOME PERMANENT CONTACT BETWEEN THE ADMINISTRATION AND THE GROUP OF PHYSICISTS WORKING ON CHAIN REACTIONS IN AMERICA.

. . . . I UNDERSTAND THAT GERMANY HAS ACTUALLY STOPPED THE SALE OF URANIUM FROM THE CZECHOSLOVAKIAN MINES WHICH SHE HAS TAKEN OVER. THAT SHE SHOULD HAVE TAKEN SUCH EARLY ACTION MIGHT PERHAPS BE UNDERSTOOD ON THE GROUND THAT THE SON OF THE GERMAN UNDER-SECRETARY OF STATE, VON WEIZSÄCKER, IS ATTACHED TO THE KAISER-WILHELM-INSTITUT IN BERLIN WHERE SOME OF THE AMERICAN WORK ON URANIUM IS NOW BEING REPEATED.

It was ten weeks before Einstein received a response from President Roosevelt, but it became clear soon enough that the President understood the importance of the revelations and suggestions from the scientist. Roosevelt concluded that the country could not risk unilateral Nazi possession of such a powerful new weapon, if indeed such a weapon could be developed. The first step was the establishment of a committee of top civilian and military officials to identify what steps should be taken toward the development of an American nuclear fission project. The seeds of the Manhattan Project had been planted.

NATURALLY OCCURRING URANIUM consists of two main isotopes—or variations—differing only in the number of neutrons in the atomic nuclei. More than 99 percent of natural uranium is uranium-238. Less than one percent of the element is the slightly less massive isotope known as uranium-235. Only the uranium-235 atoms were fissile—splitting under neutron bombardment—as in Hahn and Strassmann's 1938 experiment.

It was understood that a uranium-based atomic bomb requires a critical mass—several kilograms—of uranium-235 that is in excess of 90 percent pure. Separating the isotopes to produce the necessary *weapons-grade* uranium represented a difficult engineering challenge for America's nuclear scientists. Separation had to be based on the small mass difference between the two isotopes because they were chemically indistinguishable.

Various separation methods were considered, but one of the most successful was known as *gaseous diffusion* where compounds of uranium were vaporized and the lighter 235 components were observed to travel a greater distance inside a large closed mazelike structure where they condensed and could be collected. Construction of a large gaseous diffusion plant known as "K-25" at Oakridge, Tennessee, began in 1943. The more efficient gas centrifuges used today for isotope separation were not developed until years later.

It became clear soon enough that even the best technology available—the gaseous diffusion method for production of weapons grade uranium—was inefficient and would limit the number of uranium bombs that could be produced before the end of the War to just one or two units. But there was another material that might be employed if a new set of engineering challenges could be overcome: As early as 1934, Enrico Fermi reported the discovery of the first trans-uranium element, heavier than uranium.

In 1940 Glen Seaborg and a team of physicists at the University of California in Berkeley isolated this new element using the cyclotron at the Berkeley Radiation Laboratory. The new element was given the name *plutonium* and was determined to be fissile. More important, it was established that a nuclear reactor fueled predominantly by ordinary uranium-238 would generate large quantities of plutonium as a by-product. The plutonium produced could easily be separated from the uranium fuel.

"THERE IS LITTLE DOUBT that America and our allies will ultimately win this war. Germany may well be out of it within a year. Once that occurs, the focus will be winning the war in the Pacific." Robert Oppenheimer was addressing the senior staff at the main research facility established for the Manhattan Project in Los Alamos, New Mexico.

"But the question on the minds of the President and our military planners is this: What will be the cost of defeating the Empire of Japan? It has been estimated that an invasion of the Japanese homeland may well result in a million American casualties, plus millions more Japanese civilian and military deaths.

"Our work here has the singular purpose of ending the war earlier than would otherwise be possible. It is a curious notion, indeed, that a weapon of such unimaginable destructive power could possibly be used to save lives, but I believe it to be true. I add with no hesitation, however, that if any of you still harbor unresolved concerns regarding the morality of this endeavor, your immediate resignation from the project is encouraged and will be accepted."

THE GUN-TYPE DESIGN for a uranium bomb developed at Los Alamos was relatively simple: a "bullet" of uranium-235 is fired into a cavity in a sub-critical "receptacle" of the same material so that the combined mass instantly becomes sufficiently large to produce a self-sustaining explosive nuclear reaction. Not so with reactor-bred plutonium: when the first samples of plutonium were sent to Los Alamos from the reactor at Hanford, Washington, it was determined that the simple uranium "rifle" design could not be applied to a plutonium bomb. The reactor-bred plutonium contained a large fraction of plutonium-240 that would result in *pre-detonation* of the weapon: in the instant before the combined mass becomes critical, an excess of free neutrons would cause a partial nuclear reaction—a "fizzle"—that would blow the device apart.

Pre-detonation could be prevented only by increasing the speed at which the critical mass of nuclear material is brought together. It was determined that a uranium-style "gun barrel" would need to be dozens of feet long in order for the plutonium "bullet" to attain sufficient velocity to avoid pre-detonation. The rifle design was quickly rejected as impractical for a plutonium weapon to be carried aboard an airplane.

The solution was simple in principle, but difficult to achieve in practice: a hollow sphere of plutonium could be compressed to criticality by setting off an arrangement of explosive charges outside the sphere, instantly compressing the core to critical mass and resulting in nuclear detonation. The plutonium "implosion" bomb design was called "Fat Man." The uranium bomb was given the name "Little Boy."

President Truman was attending the Potsdam Conference of Allied leaders in July 1945 when he received word that the implosion weapon test at the Alamogordo Bombing Range, some 200 miles south of Los Alamos, was successful. He disclosed to the Soviet Premier, Joseph Stalin, that America now had "a new weapon of unusual destructive force" that might bring a quick end to the war. Stalin is said to have replied that he was "glad to hear it and hoped we would make good use of it against the Japanese."

Ironically, thanks to Soviet agents who had penetrated what had been believed to be tight security at Los Alamos, it is likely Stalin already knew about the successful American test before President Truman's disclosure.

The joint declaration of the Potsdam Conference calling for unconditional surrender of Japan was rejected by the Japanese Government on July 29, 1945. Japan hoped that the Allies would accept some sort of negotiated peace that would simply end the hostilities. On August 6, 1945, with back channel negotiations at a standstill, the B-29 Superfortress, *Enola Gay,* piloted by Colonel Paul Tibbets dropped a uranium bomb on the Japanese city of Hiroshima. Three days later, a plutonium implosion bomb was dropped on Nagasaki.

It is estimated that bombing of the two Japanese cities resulted in 200,000 deaths. No Los Alamos test of the uranium bomb had been conducted prior to its use because sufficient fissionable uranium for only a single uranium bomb had been produced by the K-25 plant at Oak Ridge by war's end.

On August 12, the United States offered terms for a Japanese surrender that would permit the Emperor to retain a role as the ceremonial Head of State. Meanwhile, additional plutonium bombs were being readied in the event that the new terms of surrender were rejected. The decision to accept the American offer was made by the Emperor himself, and a formal surrender ceremony took place aboard the battleship, *U.S.S Missouri*, on September 2, 1945.

CHAPTER SEVENTEEN

Cedarpines Park, California
October 1950

A FULL MONTH HAD PASSED since Bertrand's short excursion back in time to France in 1945. Pamela and Bertrand had moved on with their lives, and Pamela no longer harbored serious concerns about her husband's mental state.

Pamela was waiting in the car for Bertrand to come out of the house. They needed to make a trip to Goodwin's Market in town, but when Bertrand did not join her after a few minutes she sounded the horn. Finally he descended the stairs to the driveway and leaned into the passenger window, waiting in anticipation for what his wife might have to say.

"What's the problem, Bertrand? I thought you were right behind me. I've been waiting here in the car for nearly ten minutes."

"Don't be so impatient. I couldn't find my wallet." He walked around to the driver's door, but before opening it, his attention was drawn to a figure walking slowly up the road toward their house.

It was unusual to see anyone on foot along this road, and Bertrand waited with one foot on the sill of the open car door. Inside the car, Pamela was unaware of the reason why her husband was still outside the vehicle. She began to wonder if Bertrand was suffering from a renewed lapse in memory.

"Bertrand," she shouted to get his attention.

"Just a minute, Pamela, someone is coming up the road."

The approaching male figure was thin, dressed in a chamois-colored jacket and overalls, and wore sunglasses. Despite a pronounced limp, the man began to step more rapidly in Bertrand's direction. Now only fifty feet away, he removed his sunglasses and began to wave at Bertrand with his free hand. Inside the car, Pamela turned her head to see the approaching figure and cried out, "Oh my, is that my Anton?"

PAMELA REFILLED HER GRANDSON'S coffee cup and returned the carafe to the brewer before continuing her story. "He was so thin that your grandfather didn't recognize him until after I called out your father's name from inside the car."

"But why—" asked Jason, "why did it take more than five years after the War was over before he could come home?"

"I don't believe your father would have ever returned home if your grandfather hadn't followed that pigeon into the forest, but after he came home, your father told us everything. He told us about being rescued by the French Underground and later being captured by the Nazis. He was sent to an underground forced labor camp in Germany and put to work assembling the rockets that the Germans used against England.

"As a diversion from the harsh conditions, he began feeding some pigeons roosting at the prisoner's barracks. He was able to add to a note carried by a messenger pigeon, warning that a recent allied bombing raid had killed hundreds of innocent prisoners. But he had no way of knowing if anyone ever saw his message."

"So you told him that the message came to this house and about Grandfather following the pigeon into the woods?"

"Well, yes. Of course we did, but not until after he had told us the whole story. The day after he sent off that message, the Germans moved many of the workers from the rocket plant—including your father—to the south, together with some of their scientists. It was an attempt to avoid both the Russians coming from the east as well as the advancing American Army moving toward Nordhausen from the west. . . ."

"WE MUST GET YOU to the infirmary if you hope to be rescued *von den Amerikanern.*" The tactical situation for the Germans at Nordhausen had become dire in the last 48 hours and Fritz was telling Michel Depierre what he must do to save himself. "Your friend *ist im Zug*—on the train—that left one hour ago. A second transport train is being readied for the trip south. Our remaining engineers and healthy workers are to be evacuated. You will not be taken on the train if you pretend to be too sick. We can wait *auf die Amerikaner*—they are only a few kilometers away. Let us go at once."

Fritz led Michel Depierre through the deserted Mittelwerk tunnels connecting the factory assembly areas. They passed six or seven partially assembled V-1 airframes, then proceeded into a tunnel leading to the V-2 rocket engine assembly area. As Fritz heard two men approaching from a distance, he dropped back behind Michel and drew his Walther P38 semi-automatic pistol.

"Raise both your hands and keep going," he told Michel, "as if you were my prisoner." The two men coming toward them were German missile engineers, walking quickly and speaking rapidly to each other as they passed, paying scant attention to Fritz and Michel. From their conversation Fritz judged that they were worried about reaching the evacuation train before it left. "That door up ahead leads to the infirmary," Fritz told Michel.

Inside they found nine or ten patients resting in single bunks and four more bunks that were empty. Most of the patients appeared to be gravely ill and it was clear that none had been attended to for a full day or more. Michel filled two water glasses from the tap at the sink and proceeded to offer a drink to every conscious patient. Fritz stood watch at the door.

"Michel," Fritz whispered hoarsely, "get into one of the beds and cover yourself with a blanket. *Soldaten kommen.*" Michel complied immediately, resting on his back with his eyes closed.

The two soldiers who entered the infirmary were very young—probably new recruits. *"Heil Hitler, Obergefreiter,"* the two men announced in unison.

"Heil Hitler," Fritz responded. The pair seemed very nervous—more than nervous: Fritz sensed that they were frightened. "Why are you here?" Fritz barked at the men.

One of recruits stepped close to Fritz and whispered, "We have been ordered to—" he stuttered, "—to make sure no one—no one is left alive in the infirmary." The soldier rested one hand on his holstered sidearm.

"I was given the same order by Hauptmann Schmitt. I will take care of it," Fritz announced as he drew his Walther. "Are you not going to be evacuated with your unit?"

"Yes, *Obergrefreiter.*"

"Then get going. *Heraus mit Sie!*"

The young soldier closed his eyes briefly, relieved. The pair quickly exited the infirmary and Fritz closed the door behind them. He walked to the far side of the room and fired a round into the wall, waited a few seconds and fired another. He repeated the shots until the clip was empty. With each report of the Walther every conscious patient in the infirmary reacted with a startled twitch. Michel watched as Fritz loaded a fresh clip and fired a few more rounds into the wall.

MORE THAN AN HOUR passed before Fritz and Michel heard new sounds outside the infirmary door. They held their breath as the door opened slightly and the barrel of a rifle poked through. Fritz raised his hands in surrender when he realized that the soldier about to enter was not wearing a German Army uniform.

"Who are you and what's going on here?" Private John Galione posed the question, his rifle pointed at Fritz's chest. Two other soldiers followed Galione into the infirmary.

"I am Corporal Arno Bayerlein, but you can call me Fritz. These men are laborers from this camp, all in need of immediate medical attention," Fritz replied with hands still raised.

One of the American soldiers made a quickly survey of the patients in the bunks, checking for weapons. When he came to Michel, the Frenchman slowly sat up and smiled. As Galione marched Fritz out of the room, Michel called out to him. "Treat that man kindly,

Private. He saved the lives of everyone in this room."

CHAPTER EIGHTEEN

Gorodomlya Island,
North of Moscow
January 1946

THE TRAIN CARRYING the conscripted laborers from Mittelwerk—Anton Devereux among them—as well as the cadre of German rocket scientists never reached the intended destination: a complex hidden in the Austrian Alps known as the Nazi National Redoubt or *Alpenfestung*. According to Heinrich Himmler, *Reichsführer* of the SS, the Redoubt could ultimately serve as a staging point from which the Nazis could coordinate resistance groups worldwide and assure the continued existence of the Reich.

If the War was indeed lost—an opinion held by most members of the German high command—some believed that this hideout could also be a place of safety from which the last Nazi holdouts might be able to negotiate an end to the War on terms that were more favorable than the Allied demands for unconditional surrender of Germany.

But in fact, the Nazi National Redoubt was more legend than reality. While it was true that some military outposts had been established in the Southern Alps, there was no elaborate underground facility with munitions factories and stores of food sufficient to sustain up to 60,000 personnel for two years or more as some Allied intelligence reports suggested.

The rumors touting the extent of preparations in the Redoubt circulated even throughout the *Wehrmacht.* When German Field Marshall Albert Kesselring was given orders to defend the area, his men were unable to locate the vast stores of weapons and provisions that were supposedly in place; nor had any living quarters been prepared for members of the Nazi High Command in the event it should become necessary to abandon their Berlin headquarters.

Allied intelligence reports supporting the existence of the National Redoubt were bolstered by observed mass German troop movements in the direction toward the Redoubt area from the East and from the Italian Alps in the South. In fact, the German troops were simply attempting to advance toward the American lines as rapidly as possible in order to avoid capture by Soviet forces.

Over the next several days, thousands of German soldiers were able to surrender to the advancing Americans. Meanwhile, the contingent of technical personnel and prisoner workers from Mittelwerk aboard the train headed toward the hoped for German sanctuary in the South was intercepted by elements of the Soviet 3rd Army.

DESPITE THE ASSURANCES of their Soviet captors, it was not until the German scientists were shown their quarters and work spaces on Gorodomlya Island that the level of apprehension regarding their collective future began to subside. Joseph Stalin had personally ordered that the foreign weapons specialists be treated as "guest workers" and not prisoners of the long war. After all, it was argued, who else could help advance the Soviet Union into the missile age?

For Anton Devereux and the other non-Germans on the train stopped by the Soviet Army, it was only a matter of time—they believed—before the authorities identified them as Allied prisoners of the Nazis and rightfully repatriated them to their home countries. They were wrong. At the train station in Budapest all of the "guest workers"—German scientists and non-German technicians alike—were escorted to and boarded on a Soviet train that soon crossed the Hungarian frontier into the Ukraine and then on to the final destination near Moscow.

But living and working conditions for the personnel brought to Gorodomlya Island were a vast improvement over the terrible conditions at Mittelwerk: no more twelve-hour work shifts and meager rations, and although confined to an area of the island that encompassed the project buildings and housing facilities, no longer were they subject to constant surveillance and harsh supervision by brutal guards. While the guest technicians were provided with dormitory-style living quarters, the German scientists and engineers were eventually given apartments. Family members residing in Soviet-occupied zones in Germany were invited to join their scientist husbands and fathers on Gorodomlya Island.

The Soviet project leaders made sure that everyone at Gorodomlya Island understood the task that lay before them: first to duplicate for Soviet authorities the German V-2 missile design and production capability and then to develop enhancements that would greatly extend both the range and payload capacity of the German missiles. Soviet engineers and technicians were assigned to work closely with both the German scientists and non-German technicians until such time as the Soviets were able carry on the work on their own. At this point, it was promised, all of the guest workers would be sent home. Soviet planners believed that it would be four years before their own engineers could take over the work of the German rocket scientists, but that the non-German guest workers might be replaced with Soviet technicians much sooner.

The German guest workers at Gorodomlya Island were not the only scientists and engineers brought to the Soviet Union to work on Soviet military projects. Another sixty Germans and Austrians were brought to the country and interred, working on uranium isotope separation in the Soviet State of Georgia. Among them was a brilliant young mechanical engineer, Gernotte Zippe. Zippe is credited with development of a high-speed gas centrifuge that permits efficient separation of the uranium-235 isotope from common uranium samples.

"WHAT WILL BECOME OF US—to you and me—Anton?" Katrina posed the question to her boyfriend, Anton Devereux. Katrina Jungert was a German mechanical engineer who had been provided with her own apartment at the Gorodomlya Island missile complex. She and Anton met while working together on the long range missile navigation system and Anton moved in after six months. Soviet project officials neither encouraged nor discouraged such arrangements.

"What do you mean, Katrina?" Anton asked. They were seated together on the sofa, and Anton rose to turn off the television.

"The rumors that have been circulating—about the technicians—that all non-Germans may be repatriated soon. I ask you again: what will become of us?"

"If it happens, I'll insist that you be permitted to come with me."

"The Russians will never allow it; too much important work remains unfinished," replied Katrina.

"Then I will stay here and work with you until they send you back to Dresden." Anton returned to the sofa and embraced her. "I love you and I won't let them separate us." Despite his assurances, both of them understood that the prospect of their future together was largely a matter beyond their control.

CHAPTER NINETEEN

Cedarpines Park, California
Christmas Eve 1964

"THEY PUT YOUR FATHER on a train in Moscow with most of the other non-German technicians from Gorodomlya Island. When it arrived in Berlin, he was thanked for his service to the Soviet Government and escorted to the French Zone. But it was nearly a year before he came home."

"Why the French Zone? Wasn't there an American Zone in Berlin?"

"Yes, but your father had passed himself off as a Frenchman when captured by the Germans, and he thought it best to maintain the charade while working for the Soviets."

"I suppose," said Jason, "there were plenty of people interested in learning what went on at that island, but to keep him from going home for so many months after his release? That seems excessive."

"It's true—he was interviewed by some American military officials in Berlin, but no one was keeping him from coming home after his release. He made that decision on his own. It was because of that woman—Katrina. He was smitten with her and stayed in Europe, hoping that the Russians would send her home soon. He even stood in line for hours at the East German embassy in West Berlin waiting to be granted special permission to look for Katrina's family in Dresden. But the city was pretty much still in shambles from the War. He was unable to find anyone who knew the Jungert family. The entire block of homes where she grew up had been reduced to rubble."

"I read about the Allied firebombing of Dresden in my college world history class. It was pretty outrageous," offered Jason.

"Your father and Katrina were able to write to each other, but the Russians weren't ready to release her, and they wouldn't allow him back in the country to visit her. Eventually he gave up and decided to come home anyway, but you know he wasn't very happy here. It wasn't until 1953 that Katrina wrote to tell him that the Russians were finally going to send her back to Germany. He was on a boat to Hamburg ten days later, and they've been living in Leipzig ever since."

"I knew that part of it," said Jason, "and it caused a big problem for me when I applied for the job in Albuquerque."

"Why?" asked Pamela. "Why would the government care where your father was living?"

"It was because of my work. The Air Force was reluctant to issue me a security clearance when they learned my father was living in East Germany. It took several months before they cleared me."

"So you should know," said Pamela, "that I begged your father to leave East Germany with Katrina years ago. Now with cold war tensions so high—with the Berlin Wall going up and everything else—there is no way they can leave."

"THE CALL'S FOR YOU, JASON. I think it's your mother. She sounds upset." Pamela held her cupped hand over the handset so that the caller wouldn't hear her. It was the day after Christmas and Pamela had been putting away the last of the breakfast dishes when the phone rang. "Do you want to use the extension in the den?"

"No, I'll take it here." Jason took the phone from his grandmother's outstretched hand and spoke to the caller, "What's going on, Mother?"

"It's about your brother." The woman on the line was sobbing. "Two men from the Army just left the house. They told us Robert's plane crashed in Australia."

"Slow down, Mother," said Jason. "Why was he on a plane?" he paused, "And why Australia?"

"It was supposed to be a week of R and R. He left Vietnam two days ago. The plane stopped in Darwin for refueling and then headed to Sydney, but it never got there. They haven't found the plane yet. They just know it never got to Sydney."

On the other end of the line Jason could hear what sounded like his mother's phone striking the floor; then her crying in the background. The next voice he heard was that of his step-father, Paul Baker.

"Your mother and I are pretty upset here, Jason. Can you come home?"

"Yes. Of course," said Jason, "I can be there this afternoon." He hung up the telephone and backed up to the kitchen counter, leaning against it for support. Jason could see tears in his Grandmother's eyes, then looked down at the floor and folded his arms in front of his chest.

"Do you want me to help get your things together?" Pamela asked.

"Thanks, Grandma. I'm going to take a shower before I leave."

PAMELA DEVEREUX WAS SEATED at the kitchen table when Jason came back into the room. He saw his suitcase on the floor and spoke, "Thanks for packing it, Grandma."

"Paul called back while you were in the shower." Pamela continued, "Robert's plane has been found. It crashed in some rugged country west of Brisbane after a collision with a light plane. There are survivors. They just don't how many."

"We can only hope for the best," said Jason. "I'm going to leave. If I go now I can be in San Diego before dark."

"There's something else you should know, Jason." Pamela turned toward the window that looked out on the deck. "The bird—that pigeon—is back." Just outside, the young Rock Pigeon was furiously tapping on the glass with its beak. "I went out there, but he just keeps on tapping. I think he's waiting for you."

Without saying a word Jason zipped up his jacket and stepped out on the deck. As soon as he opened the door, the pigeon stopped pecking at the window glass and flew to the deck railing near the stairs that led down from the deck to the backyard. Jason stood for a moment, thinking, then turned back toward the open doorway to the kitchen and spoke to his grandmother, "This bird may be trying to lead me somewhere. If I'm not back in ten minutes, call my mother and tell her I'm going to be late."

"Be careful, Jason," said Pamela. Jason followed as the Rock Pigeon led him to edge of the woods and beyond.

JASON REMOVED HIS JACKET after thirty minutes. When he stopped to roll up his shirt sleeves, he realized it wasn't merely his activity that was causing him to sweat. It was humid, and the outside temperature was at least thirty degrees warmer than when he first started following the pigeon away from his grandmother's house.

Jason correctly assumed that the high humidity was due to the salt marshes that came into view as the forest thinned out. Now he was thankful the footpath that meandered through the marsh area was raised, keeping his feet dry. He encountered no other people along the way; the only signs of human activity were several abandoned and broken-down concrete buildings separated a few hundred feet from each other.

Twenty minutes later the buildings and salt marshes were behind him and up ahead was what appeared to be a large airbase or airport. *Maybe it's Norton Air Force Base*, Jason thought. The Norton facility was in San Bernardino, in the valley below his grandmother's house. But the expanse of blue water visible just west of the base was a problem: He knew Norton Air Force Base to be at least fifty miles from the Pacific Ocean.

The sign in front of the main gate now confirmed to Jason what he had begun to suspect. It read:

WELCOME TO ROYAL AUSTRALIAN AIR
FORCE BASE – DARWIN

"COULD I SEE SOME identification, sir?" The sentry at the main gate was polite but firm.

"Yes, of course," said Jason. He fumbled in his jacket pocket for several seconds before pulling out his Air Force Weapons Laboratory identification badge.

"What is your business here on the base?" the sentry asked.

"My brother is in the U.S. Army and was on an R and R flight from here to Sydney two days ago when his plane crashed. I'm trying to find out if he is alive or injured or . . . you know, if he didn't survive."

"I suggest you speak with someone at the Base Information Office in the next building." The sentry pointed out the location. "Someone there should be able to help you." Jason completed and signed the visitor log and was given a badge marked "RAAF Visitor - Unclassified."

Minutes later Lieutenant Hopkins in the Base Information Office listened attentively as Jason explained the reason for his visit to the RAAF Base. Hopkins looked up an entry in one of the bound log books on the counter before responding. "We get one C-130 transport on an R and R flight from Tan Son Nhut each week. It refuels here before going on to Sydney the same day. The next day it makes a return flight the same way, with American GIs who have just completed their week of R and R and are returning for duty. What day did you say your brother's plane crashed?"

"It must have been the twenty-fourth—Christmas Eve."

"That's today," said Lieutenant Hopkins. "You must have your days confused. It happens all the time crossing the International Date Line. But still, you got some bad information;

we haven't had any kind of aircraft incident here in weeks." The lieutenant looked at his watch before continuing, "The weekly R and R flight from Vietnam is due here within the hour. I can check the passenger manifest. What's your brother's name?"

"Robert," replied Jason, "Robert Baker."

JASON WAITED AT THE ARRIVAL GATE after learning from Lieutenant Hopkins that the passengers manifest indeed confirmed that one Private Robert Baker was listed as a passenger on the inbound Hercules C-130. The big plane taxied to the gate and minutes later a stream of smiling servicemen came bouncing down the rear ramp to the tarmac.

The flight schedule called for only an hour of restocking and refueling, but the passengers were happy to have a few extra minutes to stretch their legs and use a real restroom before reboarding for the last leg of their trip. The only person waiting inside the terminal was Jason Devereux.

"What the hell are you doing here, Jason?"

"It's good to see you, too, Robert." The pair of brothers sat down inside the terminal, each with a free soda and candy bar from the gedunk stand provided for military travelers, courtesy of the Royal Australian Air Force. Robert did not understand what his brother was trying to tell him.

"You expect me to believe that two hours ago you were at Grandmother Devereux's home in Cedarpines Park?" remarked Robert. "What have you been smoking?"

"Look. There's not a lot of time. They are going to call everyone back to that plane in less than an hour for the flight to Sydney. But your plane is not going to make it. There's going to be a mid-air collision with a private plane. You can't get on that flight."

"Sorry, Jason, but I've been waiting for this R and R for weeks, and you're not going to spoil it for me with some crazy speculation."

"This is nothing new; it's all happened before," said Jason.

"What's happened? What are you talking about?"

"This very strange time and location shift. It happened to Grandfather Devereux years ago. It's how my Dad was saved."

"I don't know what to tell you, Jason. Do you know what your sound like? Have they been using you as a guinea pig—testing weird shit at your laboratory in New Mexico?"

It was now clear to Jason that getting his brother to believe him was going to prove difficult. Over the next few minutes Jason provided some details of the events surrounding Bertrand Devereux's strange experience in 1950, as told to Jason by Grandmother Devereux. But he wasn't getting through to his brother. Finally, Jason shouted at Robert, "There's a free phone in the USO lounge. Call my grandmother. She can tell you all about your mother's call informing us of the plane crash."

Robert reluctantly agreed to make the call, believing there was no other way to shut his brother up.

"HELLO."

"Hi Grandma. It's Robert."

"Robert? Where are you calling from? Are you home?"

"No, Grandma. Still in Southeast Asia. I wanted to call and wish you a Merry Christmas."

"That's sweet," said Pamela.

"Have you seen Jason?" he asked.

"No, but I'm expecting him later today. Did you know he was going to spend Christmas with me here in the mountains?"

"Uh … no. What about my mother? Has she called you?"

"It's been weeks since I've spoken with her. Why do you ask? What's going on, Robert?" Robert covered the handset with his free palm and turned to Jason. "What are you trying to pull here, Jason? My mother hasn't called and Grandma says she's not expecting you 'til later today."

Jason seemed confused momentarily, but then suddenly he understood what was happening. He whispered to his brother, "Your mother won't be calling until the day after Christmas. It hasn't happened yet. Ask her . . .

ask her about her new television. It was just delivered and will prove to you I was there."

"Robert? Are you still there?" asked Pamela.

"Sorry, Grandma. Yes, I'm here. I hear you got a new TV set. Is that right?"

"Well, yes. It's my first color television—just delivered yesterday. I wanted to surprise Jason, but how did you know about it?"

"Guess I must be psychic. But I have to go now, Grandma. Say hello to Jason for me. I'll come to visit you as soon as I get back home.

"Looking forward to it. Goodbye, Robert."

Robert hung up the phone and turned to his brother. "That was kind of strange," he said. "So you get to Grandma's house and two days later my mother calls to tell you that my plane crashed. You disappear into the woods and somehow show up here in Darwin some forty-eight hours earlier? Is that what you are trying to tell me?"

"Forty-eight hours is nothing," said Jason. "Grandpa Devereux left home in 1950 and ended up in France five years before he left."

"But what's the point of this? Why would such a thing happen?"

"It's an opportunity for an alternate outcome. For Grandpa, it was a chance to save his son, my Dad. For me, it's a chance to save you—and maybe a hundred other guys—from an untimely end, but who knows why, exactly. It's a gift, and it would be foolish to disregard it, don't you think?"

"I suppose, but what now? You think we can convince anyone here to stop the flight based on your tall tale? I don't think so. And I'm getting on that plane. If it left without me and the worst happened . . . well, I'd . . . I just don't know what I'd do."

"I've got an idea," said Jason. "Give me your wallet."

THE VOICE OVER the public address system announced the reboarding call for the flight to Sydney. The soldiers filed out of the terminal building and proceeded toward the side loading ramp of the Hercules. Even at idle, the four turboprop engines were generating a lot of wind and noise. Jason waited at the terminal door, watching as the Flight Engineer checked the passes at the ramp.

"If I can just delay the take-off for a few minutes," thought Jason, *"maybe the paths of the two planes won't cross and there won't be a collision."* Jason watched closely until the last of the ninety soldiers boarded. As the Flight Engineer began to secure the side entry ramp, Jason ran toward the Hercules, shouting and waving his arms.

"Hold on there! Stop!" The Flight Engineer took notice and waited for Jason to come close.

"What's the problem?" They were shouting at each other in order to be heard over the C-130's engine noise.

"My brother's on that plane and I have his wallet. He needs it."

"Give it to me. What's your brother's name? I'll see that he gets it."

"It's Robert Baker, but I really need to give it to him myself."

"The pilot's anxious to get this crate in the air. Let me see what he says. Wait here." The Flight Engineer disappeared inside the cabin. It was a full five minutes before he reappeared with Jason's brother in tow.

"I really appreciate this," said Jason to the Flight Engineer as he thrust the wallet toward his brother. "Robert. Be sure to call your Grandmother when you land in Sydney." Robert nodded.

"Let's wrap this up, boys," said the Flight Engineer. Jason stepped back from the ramp, then turned and headed back toward the terminal building.

Robert called out, "Love ya, Jason." Jason turned his head and smiled, just in time to see his brother's face for a moment before the boarding ramp of the Hercules was drawn up and closed.

JASON TURNED IN HIS visitor's badge at the Main Gate and stepped off the base grounds. In the distance he could see the giant Hercules C-130 in the air, slowly turning to the southeast toward Sydney. All he could do now was to simply hope that the short departure delay that he caused at the airbase would be sufficient to disrupt the collision catastrophe involving his brother's transport plane.

When he reached the edge of the wetland area from which he had emerged nearly four hours earlier, he came upon a stone wall that held an information sign explaining that the concrete buildings he passed earlier were old ammunition bunkers left from World War II. Jason smiled when he noticed his traveling partner—the pigeon—perched and resting on the wall. The bird flew off a short distance as Jason approached, leading him first through the mangroves and salt marshes and then the forest of pines until they arrived an hour later at Grandmother's house.

PAMELA DEVEREUX WAS WAITING on the deck of her home when Jason emerged from the forest. The pigeon that had been Jason's guide for the last few hours flew off just as Jason set foot on the deck.

"Thank goodness you were able to save him," said Pamela.

"How do you know that?" Jason was out of breath.

"Robert called from Sydney. His plane landed safely—there was no mid-air collision. He said he had been trying to call here for the last two days. I called your mother to tell her the good news, but it was so strange. She knew nothing about a plane crash. No one from the Army had called to tell her that Robert was missing. She must have thought I was delusional. I didn't know what to do so I just apologized and hung up the phone." Pamela placed her hand on Jason's shoulder and continued, "Come into the kitchen. I'll fix you something to eat."

"SO TELL ME, GRANDMA, did Grandfather Devereux's pigeon ever return here? Did the bird lead him back into the forest ever again, for another journey into the past?"

"I saw that bird just one more time. It was the day your grandfather passed away. Your father had been home for about a year. My Bertrand was sitting on the deck in his favorite chair. I was making him a cup of tea, and I saw the bird fly down to his arm. Bertrand was smiling, gently stroking the back of the pigeon's head. I went to the closet for my jacket—I was only gone a minute—and grabbed the teacup to take it to him on the deck. He was holding that bird gently in his lap—in his two hands—but he was gone; the bird also—both were still. It was sad, but they looked so peaceful together. The doctor said it was his heart."

"Wow. One minute he was smiling, and the next he was gone? So why do you think this happened? First Grandfather saving my dad years ago, and today with Robert and me."

"I have to believe it just wasn't their time. Your father had a lot more to do with his life, and maybe Robert did also. Or maybe Robert's plane had to be saved because of someone else on it. Didn't you say there were a lot of soldiers on that flight?"

"Yes. Ninety, give or take."

"So maybe one of those men is destined for something great and had to be saved. You and that pigeon were just the means to get it done. Or maybe there is just something special about this house, or the woods, or maybe even that old aviary on the deck."

CHAPTER TWENTY

Cedarpines Park, California
June 1986

$\mathbb{A}$NTON AND KATRINA had flown in from Germany the day before the memorial service, the same day that Jason arrived from Virginia. Robert and his wife had driven from Tucson and all met at the old house in the San Bernardino Mountains.

It had been five years since Anton's last visit to California as travel to the U.S. for residents of East Germany was difficult due to prohibitions imposed by the East German Government. Six more years would pass before travel restrictions would be lifted with the reunification of East and West Germany. It was only because Anton was a U.S. citizen and the death in the family that Katrina was allowed to accompany him.

Anton and Katrina had settled into their life in East Germany after Katrina was released from her "temporary" work assignment at the Gorodomlya Island missile complex and Anton joined her in East Germany. In Leipzig, Katrina taught mechanical engineering at the local university while Anton was finally offered a job as a stocking clerk in a grocery store after unable to find any work at all for the first few years after his arrival in the country. Two years later he was promoted to cashier and recently became assistant manager of the store.

Robert attended the University of California in San Diego after his three-year army enlistment was over, met and married his wife and earned a degree in electrical engineering. They were now living in Tucson with their teenage son and daughter. Jason Devereux was married in 1970, but the marriage was over after only two years. After the divorce, he resigned from his position with the Air Force in Albuquerque and moved to Virginia, taking a job as an analyst for the Central Intelligence Agency at CIA Headquarters in Langley.

THE MEMORIAL SERVICE for Pamela Devereux was held at the Mountain Christian Fellowship Church in Crestline. Pamela was never an active member of the church body but attended from time-to-time. Julia Prince first invited Pamela to the church after Bertrand Devereux's death. After declining several invitations, she eventually accepted and came to her first service with Julia. Pamela found the services especially comforting in the first months after Bertrand's passing.

In his eulogy the Pastor told the story of Esther from the Old Testament, a brave woman of the Bible who interceded with the King of Persia to save her people from a murderous plot. He pointed to Pamela's life and her role as the strong matriarch of her family, holding out hope against all odds for the return of her only son during those desperate years during and after the War.

"She certainly was a strong woman," remarked Julia Prince. As Pamela's closest friend, Julia was invited to the Devereux home after the memorial service.

"She had to be," said Anton. "My father told me that by the end of the War, he had given up all hope that he would ever see me again, but Mother always believed in my eventual return." Katrina put her arm around her husband and kissed him on the cheek.

Robert was slicing the ham that his wife had put in the oven to bake before they left for the memorial service and called the rest of the family and Julia to the dining room.

"When do you have to go back, Pop?" asked Jason.

"We had permission to stay in the States for one week. We fly out of LAX on Thursday—first to Amsterdam on KLM; then the East German national airline, Interflug, to get home."

When the meal was over, Julia and the family stepped out to the back deck and down the stairs to the backyard. Anton carried the carton of Pamela Devereux's cremation ashes.

"Goodbye Mother. I love you," Anton Devereux spoke the words as he scattered Pamela's ashes at the tree line in the backyard of his mother's home. Years earlier, Anton and

Pamela had similarly left the ashes of Bertrand Devereux at the very same place.

"WHAT HAVE YOU been working on lately? That is, that you can tell me about." Jason Devereux and his half-brother, Robert, sat next to each other on the two most comfortable chairs on the back deck of the Devereux home. It was their first time to speak together privately since arriving from out of town.

"I can't tell you much. When I started at the Company I was an analyst in the South Asia Section. Now I supervise a half-dozen men and women that do that job. We collate data from intelligence reports, newspapers, satellite data and a few other sources and prepare assessment reports on various topics—typically military, scientific and political."

"You said 'South Asia.' What does that include?"

"Iran, Afghanistan, Pakistan, India. Mainly."

"You get to travel much?"

"Up until now, no, but I hear there might be something coming up this fall."

CHAPTER TWENTY-ONE

Afghan-Pakistan Border
October 1986

THE AGENT FROM AMERICA raised the portable missile launcher to his shoulder, demonstrating the proper firing position, and then handed it to the mujahideen commander.

"You see it's not too heavy and very easy to handle." The Commander acknowledged the statement with a nod. Six mujahideen fighters stood nearby, all paying close attention to the agent and their Commander, but with all eyes repeatedly drawn back to the wondrous new weapon on the shoulder of their Commander—a weapon they hoped would help drive the Soviet Army from their homeland.

The Soviet presence in Afghanistan began with the invasion of Kabul by a Soviet battalion of paratroopers on Christmas Day 1979. The Soviets hoped to prop up the Communist regime in control of the government that had been under attack by mujahideen insurgents. The mujahideen vehemently opposed the

Communist leadership that was attempting to shift the country away from its Muslim traditions.

The agent explained, "The missile will fly to a heat source—like the exhaust from an aircraft jet engine or a helicopter, but the missile must not be fired until you first aim it at the target heat source." The agent flipped the power switch on, then told the Commander to direct the launcher at a test bonfire set for him on a hilltop about a half-mile from their position. With the target in the viewfinder of the launcher, the system emitted an audible tone indicating that a target had been acquired—detected by the infrared sensor. "If you have the target in the viewfinder and you hear the tone, you can pull the firing trigger."

The Commander repeated the words of the agent in Pashto, the language spoken by the Afghan soldiers who had gathered around him. The agent then invited each of the men to take a turn at shouldering the weapon and directing it at the bonfire target. One of the men asked about the range of the weapon.

"Five miles," said the agent. "You may fire at an enemy helicopter or jet aircraft up to five miles away."

"In kilometers, please," requested the Commander.

"Eight kilometers." When the Commander translated, the men smiled at each other and murmured in approval.

The agent and Commander returned to the tent, open on both ends, set up near the parked Humvee that had brought the CIA training team to this location west of Tora Bora. Seated inside, Jason Devereux had been watching the demonstration. Now he addressed the Commander. "We understand that the last few months have been difficult for you mujahideen Freedom Fighters. We believe that the Stinger missiles will put you back on the offensive. Maybe in a few months the Soviets will decide it is best to leave your country."

"How many missiles can you give us?"

"Six for now, with two launchers, but we will return in three weeks with more. That is, if you have been able to use them effectively." The Commander seemed disappointed, and Jason quickly added, "Commander, please understand that each Stinger missile costs the American Government thirty-eight thousand dollars."

The Commander seemed both impressed and surprised by the value of the missiles and remarked, "When you return home, please be sure to thank your President Reagan for this generous gift."

THE SOVIET INVASION of Afghanistan had escalated cold war tensions with the United States and her NATO allies. Shortly after the 1979 incursion, President Carter ordered an embargo on grain shipments to the Soviet Union. This was followed by a U.S. boycott of the 1980 Summer Olympics in Moscow. The Soviet presence in Afghanistan was viewed as a potential threat to U.S. influence in the Persian Gulf.

From the very beginning of the incursion, the world press heralded the struggle of the mujahideen in the face of Soviet aggression. Years later, journalist and author Rob Schultheis would write, "Those hopelessly brave warriors I walked with, and their families, who suffered so much for faith and freedom and who are still not free, they were truly the people of God."

Most of the insurgent fighters were Afghans, but as the Soviet force level grew— eventually exceeding one hundred thousand troops—volunteers from neighboring Muslim countries poured into Afghanistan. Among these "Afghan Arabs" who joined in the fight against the Communist threat to Islam was one Osama bin Laden, the son of a Saudi billionaire.

CHAPTER TWENTY-TWO

Tucson, Arizona
November 3, 1986

ROBERT DIDN'T UNDERSTAND why he had been summoned to the office of the head of the Short Range Anti-Air Missile Systems Department at the Raytheon plant on Monday afternoon. This department was responsible for the "Stinger" missiles developed for use by Army and Marine Corps units, while the "Standard" missiles that Robert Baker worked on were medium and long range units deployed on U.S. Navy ships. Robert had never met Lawrence Green, the man in charge of the "Stinger" Department.

Green closed the office door before returning to his chair behind the mahogany desk. "You must be wondering what this is all about, Robert."

"Yes, sir."

"You have a brother, Jason Devereux, who is employed by a U.S. Government security agency?"

"Yes. Jason is my half-brother. We have the same mother. And I happen to know that he works for the Central Intelligence Agency."

"Very well." Green paused briefly before continuing. "You need to know that this morning we received some troubling news regarding a missile training team that was deployed to a country in Southwest Asia. Your brother is a member of that team, along with a Raytheon technician from this department. The team leader is expected to check-in with Langley every day, but it has been three days now with no contact. Satellite imagery appears to show that the team came under attack by hostile forces while enroute to a forward base of operations."

"You mean, attacked by Soviet forces, right?"

"I'm sorry, but I'm not permitted to disclose that information."

"And what about my brother? Is he OK?"

"Unfortunately, we don't have the answer to that. We know there have been casualties, but no information yet about who or even how many of the men may have been injured or killed. But it doesn't look hopeful; I'm sorry."

Robert was visibly upset. He looked down, staring at the floor. Raising his closed right hand to his mouth, he bit lightly on the knuckle of his forefinger. "When will you hear more?"

"Maybe within the next day or two. You will likely be contacted by someone from Langley, but we thought it was important to pass on what information we had." Robert just sat there, making no further response. After a minute the Department Head added, "Why don't you take a few days off? I've spoken with your supervisor about it and he agrees. When we receive any further news, we'll call you in."

ROBERT BAKER LEFT WORK early that afternoon and drove home to his family. His wife immediately discerned that he was troubled, and he lost no time explaining what he had been told concerning his brother.

"The worst part of it is the waiting—not knowing if Jason is dead or alive—and not being able to do anything about it. Maybe I should have stayed at work to wait for any news."

Ann Baker embraced her husband briefly and then stepped back, grasping his two hands with her own. "You need a distraction," she said. "Why don't you turn on the television? I'll prepare an early dinner. We just have to believe that Jason is safe."

But Robert ate very little that evening. After the dinner dishes were washed and put away they watched a pair of television sitcoms and retired early. Robert rested, but could not sleep. He lay on his back, staring at the ceiling and raising his wrist every few minutes to check the time on his watch. Shortly after midnight he slipped out of the bed taking care not to disturb his slumbering wife. He dressed quietly in the bedroom, illuminated only by the night light shining faintly through the open door of the adjacent master bathroom. Robert stepped out of the bedroom carrying his shoes and walked softly down the hallway to the family room and sat on the sofa. After a few minutes he heard the sound of his bedroom door closing.

"Why are you up, Robert?" Ann Baker had awakened and now stood at the end of the hallway in her nightgown, facing her husband at the entrance to the family room.

"Couldn't sleep," said Robert.

"Do you want me to stay up with you? Should I make some coffee?"

"No, but thanks. I know you're concerned, but I'm driving to California tonight—to the mountain house. I can be there by midmorning. Maybe there is something I can do to help my brother."

"I won't try to talk you out of it. But what should I do if you get a call from work?"

"Get a callback number and try to reach me at the house. You can leave a message on the answer phone. I'll be back in three days—four at the most."

"Will you at least call me when you get there? So I won't be worried?"

"Of course."

NO ONE FROM THE FAMILY had been to the Cedarpines Park house since Pamela Devereux passed away earlier that year. She had left the property to Jason and Robert—a tough decision for Pamela when she prepared her will. Her son

Anton was living out of the country and unlikely to return to the U.S. anytime soon, but she stipulated that he receive an equal share of the proceeds in the event that the boys decided to put the house up for sale. The fact that Robert was not really her blood grandson was never a consideration in her decision.

The property was currently under management by a local real estate agency that specialized in vacation rentals. Typically, the house might be rented for only a week or two in any given month, but even the infrequent rental payment checks represented a welcome source of extra income for Robert and his family as well as for Jason.

Robert was relieved to learn that the house was unoccupied when he arrived. The agency told him that the next scheduled rental was for a family from Palm Springs, reserving the place for Thanksgiving week.

The weather was cool and the house felt chilly inside when Robert unlocked the front door and entered. First stop was the kitchen where he tossed the deli sandwich from Goodwin's Market on the table and stowed the six-pack of beer in the refrigerator.

Robert lit the furnace pilot light—it had been off since late spring—and opened the main water valve in the corner of the basement. The water supply to the house had been secured—a precaution taken by most homeowners whenever leaving a mountain home vacant for more than a few days. A broken water pipe at an inopportune time could cost thousands in water damage as well as earning the homeowner an exorbitant bill from the local water company.

Robert hoped that he might arrive to discover a "feathered traveler" waiting for him outside on the deck near the aviary—a pigeon that might lead him through the woods to that place thousands of miles away to where his brother—unable to save himself—might be rescued. He was disappointed—not a single bird in sight. No wonder, he reasoned: it had been months since anyone had bothered to replenish the seed bowls that had for years kept the jays, finches and pigeons coming back to the aviary. They had long since learned to skip the Devereux home in their daily foraging for food.

Inside, Robert discovered a tin of wild birdseed in the cupboard above the sink along with some ground coffee. He filled the bowls in the aviary with seed while the coffee pot on the stove began to perk.

"YOU AMERICANS ARE WELCOME here for now, but do not expect it to last very long." Osama bin Laden had engaged the young CIA agent in a political discussion while sipping from the cup of tea that one of his aides had prepared for him. It was nearly dark and most of the members of the missile training team and their Saudi guests had retired for the evening. They would be leaving this camp in the morning and drive two hours to their next appointed meeting with another band of mujahideen fighters from a local tribe of Afghans.

Bin Laden understood that the missiles and training of the Afghan fighters could help achieve the goal of defeating the Soviet army, and he had volunteered to act as a trusted intermediary between the American training team personnel and the mujahideen.

"What, exactly, are you trying to tell me?" Jason Devereux posed the question to the Saudi leader.

"Take it as a warning. The mujahideen are happy to accept your gift of weapons that will help drive out the Soviet invaders. But when the Soviets are gone, you will no longer be welcome here."

"We have no intention of staying in Afghanistan," said Jason. "Our purpose here is to prevent the Soviets from extending their sphere of influence throughout South Asia and into the Middle East. My government has no interest in possessing the oil-rich lands of the Middle East, but a Soviet presence in the region would be a threat to our national security. We are here to help because it is in our own self-interest, but once the Soviets are gone, we will leave also."

"I do not believe it. You Americans cannot help yourselves from interfering where you do not belong. You call it *nation building*—bringing democracy to the ignorant and backward hordes of unfortunate natives."

"I've been in Afghanistan for only a few weeks, but the inter-tribal conflicts I have witnessed lead me to conclude that trying to establish a democratic government in this country would be like herding cats."

"That is an insulting comment. Who are you calling 'cats' and who is the 'herder'?" asked bin Laden.

"I mean no disrespect, but it would be foolish, indeed, for my country or any other to propose a Western-style government in a place where tribal law is the rule and leaders have no incentive to subordinate their power to some higher authority. It's a recipe for failure."

"It will be interesting, indeed," remarked bin Laden, "to see if the action of your government will prove consistent with or opposite to your expressed position once the Soviet invaders are driven from this land."

"Truthfully, I can offer you no assurance that my government will act intelligently in this matter. I again mean no disrespect, but what is the motivation of the foreigners such as yourself—the so-called 'Afghan Arabs'? Will you return to your homeland and allow the Afghans—once free of Soviet oppression—to govern their land as they see fit?"

"Of course, but naturally we would support a government here based strictly on Islamic Law."

"So you would be supportive of a leader such as Ahmad Shah Massoud, if he—" Jason paused to consider his choice of words carefully. "—if he were to rise to a position of leadership in the government here?"

The mention of the head of the fledgling United Front that would later come to be known as The Northern Alliance immediately raised the ire of the Saudi leader. Militants that support Massoud had successfully countered Taliban efforts to seize power in many provinces of the country.

"Massoud is a fool," said bin Laden, "and soon everyone will know that he is a traitor to both Afghanistan and Islam. He will not prevail."

"So you support the Taliban here in Afghanistan?"

"As should you. The Taliban are fighting against your enemy, the Soviets. Remember the ancient proverb that states it simply: *the enemy of my enemy is my friend.*"

"For a little while, that may be true," said Jason. Without saying another word, Osama bin Laden rose abruptly from his chair and retired to his tent.

THE SCENE WAS ONE of total devastation when the recovery team reached the site. One of the Humvees carrying the Stinger training team was blown in half; the second—with the bin Laden party—was on its side, still smoldering in the afternoon sun. There were bodies and parts strewn about, inside and on the ground outside the wrecked vehicles. No survivors.

"Looks like the Russkies caught them by surprise," remarked one of the agents in the recovery team.

His partner added, "Probably a Hind attack." The Hind MI-24 was a Soviet Attack Helicopter with an impressive suite of gun and missile weapons. Ironically, it was because of the effectiveness of the Hind and the Soviet crews of "Grey Wolves" that the Stinger training teams were first introduced into the Afghan theater.

The bodies of the three American CIA agents, including Jason Devereux, and the Raytheon technician were taken back to the CIA station east of Kandahar for eventual transport to the United States. The bodies of the bin Laden party, including Osama bin Laden, two of his wives and two aides were taken to a mountain village some ten kilometers from the attack site. They would be buried there in accordance with Muslim religious directives.

CHAPTER TWENTY-THREE

Cedarpines Park, California
November 4, 1986

ROBERT BAKER WATCHED from the kitchen table as more and more feathered visitors came to the aviary, ate their fill and then flew off. *"Probably reporting to their friends,"* he mused to himself, *"that the food kitchen at the Devereux home is open once again."*

During the preceding two hours he had consumed the deli sandwich and one of the beers from Goodwin's and most of the pot of coffee he had brewed. Dozens of birds came and went, but not a single pigeon was among them.

It was now after one PM and Robert decided he would wait no longer. He stepped out on the deck and down the stairs, stopping briefly at the tree line to look back toward the aviary. Then continued on, disappearing into the forest.

ROBERT BAKER WAS TEN MINUTES into the woods when a Rock Pigeon flew over his head, approaching from behind. It executed a tight turn in the air and then flew back, alighting on the ground behind Robert. When Robert turned and stepped back toward the bird, it flew away from him, now on the ground a few yards away in the direction toward the house. As Robert stepped closer to the bird, it continued to retreat—staying some ten feet away.

"What the hell? You're supposed to be leading me deeper into the woods—not back to the house." Robert chuckled to himself with the realization that he had spoken the words out loud—with only a pigeon to hear him. He turned and proceeded along the path further into woods, now ignoring the bird as it took short hops in his direction, following a few feet behind.

It was a half-hour later before Robert became aware that the pigeon was no longer behind him. The dense growth of pines had thinned considerably, and up ahead the terrain was rocky and treeless.

HE HEARD THE TWO HUMVEES before they came into view at the top of a rise on the dirt road up ahead. Robert stopped and raised both arms with hands open when he saw someone in the lead vehicle pointing a long-barreled weapon in his direction.

The first Humvee slowed and came to a full stop fifty feet from Robert. Two men stepped out of the vehicle—one from each side. Neither was in uniform, but each had an automatic weapon trained on Robert as they approached him. A third man exited the Humvee. It was Jason Devereux.

"Who are you and what are you doing out here?" asked one of the armed men.

Robert answered with hands still raised, "My name is Robert Baker. Jason Devereux is my brother."

"It's OK, guys," Jason yelled as he ran past the two armed agents. "He *is* my brother. How—what. . . what are you doing here, Robert?"

"It's a long story."

"I'm listening." When the two agents realized that the stranger who called himself 'Robert' was not a threat, they returned to the Humvee and stowed their weapons inside. One of men walked back to the bin Laden party to explain the situation.

"Would you believe me, Jason, if I told you that two hours ago I was at the house in Cedarpines?"

"Sure. I can believe it. This part of Afghanistan is not on the list of popular tourist destinations." Jason continued, "So you followed a pigeon into the woods behind the house and ended up here?"

"Not exactly. The pigeon followed me—for a while, anyway. What's important is that I'm here and your little convoy is in danger." Robert paused for a few seconds. "No, it's worse than that. Very soon—maybe today—you'll be attacked by some Soviet units operating in the area."

"How do you know that?"

"The head of the Stinger department at my plant in Tucson told me. Someone in your group was to stay in contact with Langley. When you went dark for a few days, they redirected a satellite. I didn't see the photos, but they said there was a lot of wreckage."

"Do you know where we get hit?"

"No. Just somewhere on the road to your next training session."

"That could be in the next fifteen minutes. Did they say if the attack came by air or ground?"

"They didn't say."

"Not helpful. If it was—or rather, is—ground units, we're basically screwed. We may be able to deal with one or two attack helicopters."

"Jason, why not head back to a safe zone, or whatever you call it? Or just hang out here for a day or two before moving out?"

"I'll defer to the other agents, or maybe the Arab. They're familiar with the threat. I don't know jack when it comes to hostile engagement."

"What Arab?"

"He's some rich Saudi—in the second Humvee with his entourage. He's opened a few doors for us with the locals. We'll handle the situation the best we can. Why don't you get the hell out of here? Head back to the house."

"Not happening. As I recall, you were shuffling papers in Albuquerque while I was dodging bullets in Vietnam. You need me here."

"And what do you propose to tell the other men in my crew?"

"About?"

"About how you got here—and why."

"Just tell them I'm a contractor for the military. It's true, I am. And that I was told that some Soviet units were operating in the region where my brother's team was conducting missile training operations. I was worried so I tracked you down."

"So you just showed up here somehow—on your own?"

"No. Look around. Plenty of mountain villages around here. We'll tell them my team volunteered to work with some local farmers for a few days—helping solve their water problems. You know—good will and public relations. We knew where you were training yesterday and that you were headed west on this dirt road. I've been waiting for you to get here."

"Let's just hope you won't have to go into any detail."

THIRTY MINUTES LATER the two-vehicle caravan continued toward the next training destination. Robert Baker rode with his brother in the first Humvee. Except for the drivers, the men in both vehicles continuously scanned the landscape and the skies with binoculars, looking out for any possible hostile troops or aircraft. As a precaution, a Stinger launcher and two missiles were unpacked and readied for action inside each vehicle.

As they pressed on the condition of the road degraded precipitously, and the vehicles were now moving forward at barely a crawl. The lead Humvee stopped abruptly when one of the men inside observed some activity in the distance: a pair of helicopters could be seen low in the sky more than a mile away, slowly crossing above the road on which the caravan was traveling.

"We have no air assets in the region," remarked one of the agents. "Those are probably Soviet attack helicopters. If they have seen us and turn in our direction, we're going to have to engage them." The two brothers simply turned and looked at each other.

"If we hadn't stopped to pick up Robert, we probably could have reached a point on the road up ahead just in time to see those helicopters up close. Damn," the driver commented sarcastically.

The tension level inside the Humvee remained high until the two helicopters slowly disappeared beyond the horizon to the west. "Thankfully, gentlemen, it appears that we may have just dodged a bullet—or two," said Jason.

The driver smiled and restarted the engine, but before engaging the drive, Robert spoke up. "Hold on a minute. I'm getting out."

"What? Why?" asked Jason.

"The threat is passed, and I'm going home— I mean, back to the village."

"We have some time; we can take you," said the driver.

"No. It's only a couple of miles. I'll be OK." As Jason exited the vehicle, he added, "Take care, Jason. Hope to see you soon."

THE PATH THAT ROBERT had followed out of woods less than two hours earlier was easy to find. As he retraced the trail back into the thick of the woods, he felt pleased with himself, confident that his travel that day in time and space had averted the attack on the small caravan, saving not only his brother but the lives of several other Americans and a contingent of Arab fellow travelers.

But his general feeling of overall well-being ended abruptly when he came upon the pigeon on the ground in the middle of the path. It was just a few feet ahead of him. Without warning, the bird flew up into his face with claws extended. Then as quickly as it appeared, the bird was gone. Robert raised his hand to his forehead, then looked at the smear of blood on his fingers.

He was scratched up, but not seriously injured. Robert wondered to himself, *"What is the problem with that bird? I thought we were on the same team."* But he thought little more about it once he emerged from the forest and into the yard behind the Cedarpines Park house. Robert called home and told his wife that all was well, and that he would be leaving for home in the morning.

CHAPTER TWENTY-FOUR

Vienna, Austria
November 1997

"SO YOU WERE BORN in the Czech Republic?" The reporter from *Der Spiegel* had come to Vienna to interview Doctor Gernot Zippe on the occasion of his eightieth birthday. Zippe agreed to meet with the reporter at a quiet coffee house in the City.

"Yes, but in 1917 it was part of Austria-Hungary."

"How is it, then, that you that you served in the Luftwaffe?"

"I was studying mechanical engineering here in Vienna before the War. By the time I graduated, half of Europe had become part of the German Empire. I was a flight instructor for a time, but after completing my graduate degree, I was sent to Munich to work on isotope separation for the German nuclear weapons project."

"That's interesting. I was unaware that Germany had a nuclear weapons program during World War Two." Apparently, Zippe's statement was a revelation to the young reporter, and she stopped her note taking briefly.

"If you had done your research, you would know that nuclear fission was discovered by German scientists in the 1930s. Serious work in developing a bomb began in 1939 under such notable physicists as Walther Bothe, Otto Hahn and Werner Heisenberg. But the German efforts were compromised by the government's own policies: Many young German physicists were simply drafted into the army as foot soldiers, and dozens of talented and experienced Jewish theoretical physicists left Europe for America even before the War began. The list included Albert Einstein, Edward Teller and Leo Szilard. Even Enrico Fermi left a prestigious position at the University of Rome after new Italian racial laws were passed that would impact his family; Fermi's wife was Jewish."

"Wasn't it Albert Einstein who alerted the American president that a bomb might be developed?" the reporter asked.

"Yes. He wrote a letter to Roosevelt in 1939, and the other scientists that I mentioned were critical to the success of the American Manhattan Project. If America had completed bomb development before the war in Europe was over, I have no doubt it would have been used against the German homeland, and Germany would have only it's own radical anti-Jewish policies to blame. Remember, too, that it was an American-born Jew—Robert Oppenheimer—who became known as the 'father of the atomic bomb' for his management of the Manhattan Project."

"So how close was Germany to developing a bomb?"

"Not very close, as it turned out. By 1942 the German High Command realized that no bomb could be developed in time to affect the outcome of the War. Nuclear research work continued, but at a slower pace, while resources were poured into more mature weapons programs like missiles and jet aircraft development."

The reporter had resumed her note taking. During the interlude while she wrote, Zippe signaled the server to bring two more espressos.

"I want to hear more about your work, Doctor Zippe. Your high-speed centrifuge designs—they were developed in Munich?"

"The initial concepts—yes—in Munich, but as I mentioned before, it was so late in the War that my invention was of no real benefit to the German war effort. But someone must have recognized the potential. I was living in the Soviet Zone—what later became East Germany—when I was kidnapped off the street by some Soviet agents."

"Really? That must have been a harrowing experience."

"Harrowing? That doesn't nearly describe it. I believed at first that I was about to be murdered. But my captors assured me that I would not be harmed. I didn't believe them until I arrived at their research facility in Tbilisi. Over the next ten years I worked on high-speed centrifuge designs for uranium isotope separation."

"And then?"

"And then I was allowed to return to my home in Vienna." The reporter made a few more notes and then began to gather her papers together.

"Thank you so much for your time today, Doctor Zippe. I have just one more question for you, if you can answer it."

"That sounds ominous," he reflected, "what is it that you want to know?"

"I have read that your invention—the high-speed gas centrifuge—has contributed significantly to nuclear arms proliferation. Do you have any thoughts—any response—to this charge?"

Gernot Zippe thought for a moment before replying. Finally he said, "With a kitchen knife you can peel a potato or kill your neighbor; it's up to governments to use the centrifuge for the benefit of mankind."

CHAPTER TWENTY-FIVE

Dimona, Israel
December 2010

"EVEN IF WE CAN GET this computer worm to work, how can we possibly hope to plant it in the Iranian centrifuge network?" The young computer engineer posed the question to his supervisor, Ephraim Gold.

"That's not our concern here, Moshe," replied Ephraim. "We do our part, and there are others who will do there's. It is as simple as that."

Ephraim Gold was a child holocaust survivor who was sent to live with distant relatives in Australia after World War Two. Ephraim's parents and older sister had perished in the Nazi death camp at Treblinka.

From an early age he exhibited an unusual aptitude for mathematics and studied computer science at the University of Brisbane, earning a doctorate. He was also interested in flying and took student pilot lessons at a local flight academy after completing his computer studies.

But Ephraim's fascination with flight was short-lived. During his very first solo flight the Cessna trainer he was piloting barely avoided a mid-air collision with an American military transport. He simply failed to notice that he had drifted into the path of the transport while climbing to altitude. Shaken, he landed safely at the flight academy airstrip and immediately announced to his instructor that he was no longer interested in obtaining his private pilot's license.

Ephraim immigrated to Israel after the 1967 Six-Day Arab-Israeli War and enlisted in the IDF (Israel Defense Forces). He had hoped to serve in an army brigade, but officials recognized his unique academic credentials and assigned him instead to the IDF Science Corps. After his IDF service term came to an end, Ephraim joined the staff at the Negev Nuclear Research Center, an Israeli nuclear installation in the Negev Desert. The Center managed the nuclear reactor nearby at Dimona, believed to be the source of the weapons-grade plutonium used for the weapons in Israel's nuclear arsenal.

Ephraim spent twenty years helping to develop Israel's nuclear arsenal before returning to Australia with his Israeli wife and two children. Ephraim welcomed the opportunity to teach and conduct research in scientific computing at his former alma mater in Brisbane.

THE STRANGER WAS WAITING outside the classroom in the Computer Sciences Building when the class bell rang. It was five minutes before the last of the students emerged from Professor Gold's class, followed by the Professor himself.

"Doctor Gold?"

"Yes, can I help you?"

"My name is Ehud Bergdorf. Could I impose on you for a few minutes?" The Stranger was much younger than Professor Gold and spoke with a noticeable accent.

"I suppose."

"Is there somewhere we could speak privately?"

"I'm going to my car. Would that work?" Ehud gestured for the Professor to lead the way.

In the reserved section of the parking lot Professor Gold unlocked the doors to his late model sedan, and the two men entered the vehicle.

"What is this about, Mister Bergdorf?"

"First, let me thank you for agreeing to speak with me." Ehud paused briefly before continuing. "You have probably guessed that I am from Israel." Professor Gold nodded in acknowledgement. "I work for a special agency of—of the Israeli Government and have been sent here specifically to request your assistance in a matter of vital security interest to the State of Israel."

"That's a long way to come to speak to a university professor. Please continue, Mister Bergdorf."

"Unfortunately, I have not been advised as to the exact nature of the project for security reasons, but I will tell you what I can. As you probably know, there has been increasing concern in our country—excuse me, Professor—in *my* country regarding the development and possible deployment of weapons of mass destruction by the Islamic Republic of Iran. Our best experts have concluded that without some external intervention, Iran will likely have a nuclear weapon and a missile delivery system capable of striking Tel Aviv within a few short years. That must never happen. Yet it seems that our friends in the West are reluctant to apply enough economic and political pressure to keep it from happening. The American and European threats for more severe sanctions or possible military intervention seem empty."

"I understand, Mister Bergdorf, and I agree with your premise. You may have heard the popular saying of a past American President. It was Theodore Roosevelt who said, "Walk softly and carry a big stick." In contrast, Western politicians dealing with the Iran problem seem to talk quite forcefully, but there is little real power behind the words."

Professor Gold continued, "But understand that I left Israel more than twenty years ago and have not been back. My early work has long since been surpassed by your scientists who came after me. I don't believe there is much I can do to help. Besides, I have a career here at the University and my family—you know. . . ."

"Professor Gold, you are a world-recognized computer software expert and spent years helping Israel with uranium enrichment. This special project deals with both of those subjects and could likely be completed in a few months. We would arrange a sabbatical leave for one school semester at Haifa University. You would be paid well, and your family could come to visit at mid-term. But most important, success of this project would be of inestimable value to the State of Israel."

"I AM CONFIDENT that the development phase of our special project will be complete by the end of this month." Ephraim Gold was briefing top staff members in the Technology Department of the agency that recruited him.

The "Special Project" was a computer software worm designed to exploit vulnerabilities in the software that controls operation of the P-2 gas centrifuges used for uranium isotope separation.

The P-2 design was the brainchild of a prominent Pakistani metallurgical engineer, Abdul Qadeer Khan. After the 1971 war between Pakistan and India, the Pakistani government initiated a crash program to develop an atomic bomb, and Khan joined the program in 1974. The program was accelerated after India conducted its first successful atomic test code-named *Smiling Buddha*. The Indian weapon was an implosion device using just six kilograms of plutonium.

Based upon the Zippe-type gas centrifuges, Khan's P-2 design utilized high-strength materials for the centrifuge rotors that permitted them to spin at speeds up to 100,000 revolutions per minute, far faster than any earlier designs. The high speed enabled more efficient uranium enrichment.

Pakistan conducted its first successful test of a uranium bomb on May 28, 1998, followed two days later by a plutonium device. Clearly, Pakistan's atomic bomb development had proceeded along two independent design paths in a manner similar to the American Manhattan Project.

Khan had access to the original Zippe designs while working for a subcontractor hired by a European uranium enrichment company known as URENCO. It has been postulated that URENCO administration officials authorized Khan to take blueprints of the Zippe centrifuges to Pakistan.

Within a few years, P-2 style centrifuges were spinning in North Korea, Libya, China and Iran. North Korea traded ballistic missile technology to Pakistan for the P-2 design. Critical nuclear technology was also sold or traded by Khan outside the purview of the Pakistani Government through what has come to be known as the A. Q. Khan Network.

Inspections conducted by the International Atomic Energy Agency revealed the existence of a formerly secret large enrichment facility in Iran using centrifuges similar to the P-2 designs, believed to have been obtained from URENCO. By 2010, several thousand advanced gas centrifuges were operating at the Natanz Nuclear Facility in central Iran.

"YOU ARE CERTAIN that this is the device that you found two weeks ago?" The Security Officer at Natanz was interrogating the computer engineer in his cubicle inside the building housing the nuclear facility's Centrifuge Complex. The device of interest was a computer thumb drive that the engineer had removed from his desk drawer and handed to the Security Officer.

"Yes, I'm sure."

"Where, exactly, did you find it?"

"It was lying on the footpath leading from the parking lot, and I picked it up," replied Ahmad, the engineer. The Security Officer turned the piece over, taking note of the Natanz facility logo that was silk-screened on the device. "I assumed that one of the other engineers had dropped it on his way into the building," added Ahmad.

"And what did you do with it?"

"I first asked if anyone in the office had lost it, but no one admitted to it so I inserted it into the USB port on my workstation." The engineer pointed to his desktop personal computer—a personal computer of Chinese manufacture with a Windows operating system. "I first scanned it with our anti-virus software, finding nothing malicious or even suspicious. So I opened the drive to examine the file contents. I thought that one of files might tell me who it belonged to."

"What did you discover in the files?"

"Just a few technical documents, nothing classified. Mostly in Persian and Arabic, and one doctoral thesis on nuclear binding energy, in English. They were in PDF format and had probably been previously downloaded from the internet. But there was nothing to tell me who it belonged to."

"Ahmad, I must inform you that a similar device was found at the Fordow facility." The security officer continued in a stern voice, "And a technician at that location took similar action as you have done here. Unfortunately, it now seems clear that the two of you are responsible—through your negligence—for releasing a computer virus that has caused the destruction of more than one thousand of our most advanced gas centrifuges inside each of the two facilities. Congratulations," the Security Officer added sarcastically.

"I am truly sorry, sir." Ahmad covered his face with his hands.

CHAPTER TWENTY-SIX

Cedarpines Park, California
November 2004

JASON HAD FLOWN to Tucson to spend a few days with his younger brother, and the two of them drove from there to Crestline to sign the final escrow papers for the sale of the Cedarpines Park house. It had been three years since either of the brothers had visited the property, and they agreed that it was time to dispose of it.

The buyers had made an offer that was well below the listing price, but the real estate agent—from the same office that had been handling the vacation rental of the property—explained that the economic downturn following the 9/11 attack three years earlier had caused many potential home buyers to delay their purchase plans. Only in the last few months had the real estate market for inland California communities begun to return to the previous level of activity.

The purchase offer was the only one they received since listing the property eight weeks earlier. After considering the offer they decided to accept it.

Jason's father, Anton Devereux, had passed away in Germany seven years earlier—following just one month after the death of his wife, Katrina. Jason did not attend his father's funeral. When Robert asked his brother about it while in San Diego a year later, Jason admitted that he had never been very close to his father.

"It wasn't really his fault." Jason explained, "The War and all those years he was interred afterwards had a big impact on him. We had only a short time together before he went back to Germany."

"Do you ever wish it had played out differently? Maybe if he and Katrina had left Germany and moved to the States?"

"Who knows? We were never close, but I didn't blame him. And after all these years I don't feel differently about it."

As the brothers left the real estate office, Robert brought up a subject that had been bothering him for several days—ever since he learned from a recent news report that Al Qaeda, under the leadership of Osama bin Laden, had claimed responsibility for the 9/11 attacks on the World Trade Center and the Pentagon. The claim was made on a video tape featuring bin Laden that was aired by Al Jazeera on October 29, 2004.

"The leader of those Arabs—the ones who were assisting you with Stinger missile training for the mujahideen fighters in 1986—he's the same bin Laden who has been all over the news the last couple weeks; isn't he?

"One in the same," said Jason. "Osama bin Laden's group was also responsible for the embassy bombings in Africa and the bombing of the *U.S.S Cole* in Yemen in October 2000."

"So it's true? We avoided an attack from those Soviet helicopters in Afghanistan because they never detected our two-vehicle caravan. All of us—including Osama bin Laden and his party—were saved."

"You remember," said Jason, "that my team was traveling to the next missile training location when you showed up. Your visit delayed us long enough to miss the encounter with the Soviets. If you hadn't arrived when you did, I probably wouldn't be here today."

"True," said Robert, "but that bin Laden character wouldn't have been around either. Without his leadership maybe those Al Qaeda attacks, including 9/11, may never have occurred."

"WELCOME, GENTLEMEN. COME IN. I'm Sue Henderson. My husband, Tim, is down in the basement poking around. I think he needs your help." Sue and Tim Henderson—the buyers—had completed the final walk-through of the property the day before and asked their agent if Jason and Robert could come by the house. The new owners had a few questions concerning the property. "We're from Palm

Springs," she said, "and mountain living is a brand new experience for both of us."

"Not a problem, Mrs. Henderson. It gives Robert and me a chance to see the old homestead one more time. I hope we can be of help."

The brothers spent the next hour with the new owners explaining some of the finer points concerning the property: They showed the Hendersons the water supply shut-off valve and explained why it was important to secure the water if they were going to leave for a few days—especially if freezing temperatures were expected. The yellow stain that Sue Henderson noticed in the tap water was due to rust in the galvanized pipes—it would go away, Jason told them, once the plumbing was in use for a few days. Someday, they might want to replace all the water lines with copper. Outside the house, Jason was able to locate the stakes that Grandfather Devereux had used to mark the corners of the property seventy years before. They were found buried under several seasons' accumulation of fallen autumn leaves.

During the course of their discussion, Robert learned that Tim Henderson had spent thirteen months in Vietnam during that war. It was more than a year after Robert had returned home from his service. Tim added that his twenty-one years old son in the Marine Corps had recently deployed to Afghanistan.

"We haven't decided what to do with the deck," said Tim. "The support timbers seem to be in good shape, but we'll probably need to replace the surface planks and railings before long."

"And probably the stairs down to the back yard," added Jason. Sue Henderson had made a pot of coffee and the four of them were seated around the kitchen table.

"After the walk-through yesterday, Sue and I decided that the aviary had to go—it's in pretty bad shape. But we put out some birdseed this morning; maybe I'll repair it instead. We've enjoyed watching the birds coming and going all morning."

"Yes," added Sue Henderson. "They come *and* go—all of them except for that one pigeon." Sue pointed toward the deck. A young Rock Pigeon was on top of the aviary, facing the kitchen window, as if he were observing the humans who were watching him from inside. "He's been there all morning—either on top of the aviary or sitting on the window sill, pecking at the glass." At her words, the two brothers turned toward each other, their eyes meeting momentarily.

"You know," said Jason, "throughout the years we've had some visitors—some very special pigeons like the one outside—coming to this house. If you have the time, we'd like to tell you some stories I'm sure you'll find interesting. . . ."

AUTHOR'S NOTES

EXCEPT FOR THE BRIEF EXCURSIONS into post-war alternative history depicted in this novel, the important events included as a part of the storyline are believed to be historically correct. The reader need not be reminded, of course, that this is a work of fiction. The experiences described and dialog of both the ordinary and historically important persons included here should be considered as products of the author's imagination and are in no way intended to reflect the true character, actions, conversation or opinions of these individuals. The following information is presented in order to amplify or correct details that were presented as part of the storyline.

- Michel Depierre was born at Villers-Vermont, France, in 1926. While the story account suggests that he became a member of an existing resistance cell sometime before August 1943, he did not join the French Resistance Movement until D-Day—June 6, 1944. Depierre was arrested by the Gestapo on July 20,

1944, and was later sent to the Mittelbau Dora concentration camp where he was put to work assembling the Nazi V-1 and V-2 weapons. Despite the harsh conditions, he survived and was eventually rescued by American forces in April 1945. In 1999 Depierre wrote about his experiences in the Resistance, his arrest and imprisonment and eventual liberation by U.S. Army personnel.[1]

• Ken Stone was a Ball Turret Gunner (BTG) on a B-17 Flying Fortress assigned to the 381st Bombardment Group at Ridgewell, England. Stone held the rank of Staff Sergeant and completed 25 combat missions over German-occupied Europe between June 1943 and January 1944. B-17 bomber crews were required to complete 25 air combat missions before being reassigned to duty in the United States. Later in the war, the minimum required number of missions was raised from 25 to 35.

By his own account, Stone regarded his 16th mission, the bombing of a critical German ball bearing factory at Schweinfurt on August 17, 1943, as his "roughest" mission. Of the 26 aircraft dispatched in the raid, his B-17 "Big Time Operator" was one of only fifteen bombers that returned to base.[2]

- Private John M. Galione and two other soldiers from the U.S. 104th "Timberwolf" Army Infantry Division entered the Mittelbau Dora work camp early in the morning of April 11, 1945. Elements of the U.S. Third Armored Division and Galione's 104th Division were notified by radio. Medics summoned to the camp discovered some 1,200 malnourished prisoners as well as the bodies of more than 5,000 dead.

  Galione's discovery was also responsible for alerting U.S. Command officials of the existence of the Mittelwerk missile production facility and making it possible for the missile hardware and technology to fall under American control. [3]

- Wernher von Braun and most of his cadre of rocket scientists and engineers were able to surrender to elements of the U.S. military in Austria at the end of World War Two. He and his team members were brought to the United States in September and October 1945 as part of Operation Paperclip, an initiative that was not publicized due to its politically sensitive nature: the notion that Germans—some of them with Nazi party affiliation—who were responsible for the V-2 missiles and the destruction they caused might somehow be absolved of their past bad deeds and brought to America was a source of consternation among many U.S. government officials.

In the end, the perceived value that the German scientists and engineers might bring to America's nearly non-existent missile programs trumped every political concern. The team was sent to White Sands Proving Ground in New Mexico where several captured V-2 missiles were tested under government direction.

In 1950 von Braun and his team were transferred to Redstone Arsenal in Huntsville, Alabama, where the Redstone and Jupiter-C rockets were developed. The Jupiter-C launched Explorer 1, America's first artificial satellite, into earth orbit on January 31, 1958. Von Braun developed and proposed several plans for space exploration, including an orbiting space station, a base on the Moon and a mission to Mars. Although he failed to convince government planners to proceed with these projects, he nonetheless received much public support for his space exploration ideas.

In 1960, von Braun became the Director of the National Aeronautics and Space Administration (NASA). At NASA he managed both Saturn rocket development and the Apollo moon landing program. The Saturn V eventually carried American astronauts on six successful missions to the lunar surface.

Von Braun resigned as Director of NASA in 1970 and later left government service to become Vice President for Engineering and Development at Fairchild Industries in Germantown, Maryland. Wernher von Braun died from pancreatic cancer in June 1977. [4,5]

- Gorodomlya is an island on Seliger Lake, about 200 miles northwest of Moscow. Prior to the 1900s it was the site of monasteries established by Russian Orthodox and (later) Ascetic monks. The Soviet government evicted the monks in 1928 and established a biological research facility on the island. The Soviet Ministry of Armaments designated it a branch of the Podlipki Rocket Development Institute to be staffed by former German rocket scientists, including many who had worked at the Peenemünde Army Research Center and Mittelwerk near Nordhausen.

Except for a few German electronics engineers who were offered employment contracts with the Soviet military, most of the German workers and their families were returned to their homes in Germany by November 1953. There is no evidence to suggest that non-German technicians from Mittelwerk were ever taken to Gorodomlya Island to work on Soviet missile programs.[6]

- Construction of the Israeli nuclear facility at Dimona began in 1958 with reactor equipment and technical support provided by France. Israel initially claimed that the reactor was a relatively low power unit that would be used strictly for peaceful research purposes. Prime Minister David Ben-Gurion suggested that the reactor would provide power necessary for a planned high-capacity desalinization plant. In fact, the reactor was a particularly large unit— perhaps up to 60 megawatts output— capable of producing more than 20 kilograms of plutonium per year.

It was more than two years later that the true nature of the Dimona facility was revealed after a visit by a University of Michigan professor consulting for the Israeli Atomic Energy Commission. Despite pressure from the U.S. Government, Israel was able to obtain heavy water from Britain and uranium from Gabon and Argentina sufficient to embark on a nuclear weapons program.

It has been a long-standing Israeli policy to never admit to possession of nuclear weapons of any kind, but intelligence sources estimate that Israel may have up to 300 such weapons in a variety of configurations including ballistic and cruise missile warheads, gravity bombs, nuclear land mines, tactical (artillery) warheads and even suitcase bombs.[7]

- Stuxnet is the name given to a computer worm designed to exploit vulnerabilities in a particular class of Programmable Logic Controllers—devices that control the operation of mechanical or electronic hardware. The worm is typically loaded into a networked computer from a flash drive and searches throughout the network for software that runs the controllers.

Stuxnet consists of three main modules including worm routines that rewrite controller instructions to induce damage to critical hardware elements, a link file that propagates and runs copies of the worm, and a module responsible for hiding all malicious files and processes to prevent discovery of the malware.

The Stuxnet worm was first identified in June 2010. It is estimated that infected controllers were responsible for the destruction of up to a thousand gas centrifuges at the Natanz Nuclear Facility in Iran. The worm modifies the control instructions, causing the centrifuge rotors to first exceed their safe design speed of rotation and then run slowly for a period of time. The speed change is responsible for differential expansion of components, causing vital mechanical parts to come into contact with each other, destroying the device. Although much information remains unsubstantiated, it has been suggested that Stuxnet was developed by the U.S. National Security Agency in collaboration with elements of the Israeli government.[8]

• After several years developing and perfecting his gas centrifuge design for the Soviets, Gernot Zippe was allowed to return to Vienna in 1956. Although Zippe was not permitted to take design documents out of the Soviet Union upon his release, he was able to reproduce his prior work from memory while temporarily working under a government contract arranged through the University of Virginia. Subsequently, he worked as a paid consultant to several Asian foreign governments.

- Early U.S. initiatives at isotope separation using gas centrifuges had been abandoned during the Manhattan Project due to technical difficulties. Today, most uranium isotope separation activity throughout the world uses gas centrifuges based on Zippe's designs. Gernot Zippe died in Munich, Germany, in 2008 at the age of ninety.[9]

- Osama bin Laden was one of 54 children fathered by the founder of the Saudi Bin Laden Group, a multi-national construction conglomerate with headquarters in Jeddah, Saudi Arabia. After his 1979 graduation from King Abdul Aziz University, bin Laden worked in the family business until the Soviet invasion of Afghanistan. He raised money for the mujahideen Afghans and often participated with them in military engagements against the Soviets.

  After the Soviet departure from Afghanistan, bin Laden returned to work in the family business until coalition forces invaded Iraq in 1990. He was the founder of Al Qaeda (meaning "the base") and often expressed outrage that U.S. forces were stationed near Muslim holy sites at Mecca and Medina.

It is believed that bin Laden directed the attacks on the World Trade Center in New York (1993 and 2001), the "Blackhawk Down" incident in Mogadishu, Sudan (1993), attack on the Khobar military base in Saudi Arabia (1996), truck bombing of American embassies in Kenya and Tanzania (1998), bombing of the *U.S.S. Cole* (2000), and other attacks—as well as several failed attempts—directed against American personnel and facilities.

Bin Laden often issued his orders or statements through audio or video tape addresses. When no new tapes were disclosed for a time after 2002, it was reported that he may have been killed in a directed bombing raid or succumbed to kidney failure due to unavailability of dialysis treatments upon which he was dependent. The reports proved to be unfounded.

On May 2, 2011, a U.S. military team that included Navy Seals stormed what was believed to be the bin Laden compound in Abbottabad, Pakistan. Bin Laden was killed along with four other inhabitants of the compound. There is no evidence to support rumors that Osama bin Laden operated in conjunction with the Central Intelligence Agency during the years of Soviet occupation in Afghanistan.[10,11]

- Ahmad Shah Massoud was regarded as one of the most effective leaders of the Afghan resistance during the 1980s Soviet occupation. He was known by his followers as the "Lion of Panjshir." After the Soviet departure from Afghanistan in 1989, the Northern Alliance under Massoud's leadership represented the chief military opposition to the Taliban. Massoud supported the notion that Afghanistan should become a more pluralistic society with a democratic form of government rather than following the strict dictates of Talifban-supported Sharia.

Two days before the 9/11 attacks on America, Taliban agents posing as reporters seeking an interview with Massoud exploded a bomb hidden in a video camera, killing the anti-Taliban leader. It is generally believed that the suicide attack on Massoud was carried out in anticipation of the expected response from the United States after 9/11. The Taliban understood that the Northern Alliance would likely support U.S. efforts to defeat the Taliban in Afghanistan, and crippling the local opposition by assassination of its leadership was considered a tactical imperative. [12]

- George S. Patton was a 1909 graduate of West Point and first saw military action in 1915 against Mexican insurgents led by Pancho Villa. He became an expert in tank warfare in Europe during World War I. Patton proved himself as a skilled tactician and military leader during World War II with successes in North Africa, the invasion of Sicily, and his spearhead drive across Northern France and into Germany as the general in charge of the U.S. Third Army.

  Patton's reputation as a military leader was clouded with controversy. He often expressed opinions that conflicted with the official position of the War Department and the Supreme Allied Commander, General Dwight Eisenhower. Patton distrusted the Soviets and predicted the post-war problems that later arose with that powerful wartime ally. He was relieved of command in October 1945 for engaging in public criticism of new de-Nazification policies.

  George Patton was seriously injured in an automobile accident in December

1945 and died in a hospital in Heidelberg, Germany, twelve days later. A few published accounts began to appear some thirty years later suggesting that Patton's death was not an accident, but an assassination. In a 2008 book, *Target: Patton*, military historian Robert Wilcox claims that George Patton's assassination was ordered by the U.S. Office of Strategic Services (OSS) and carried out with the assistance of a Soviet agent.[13,14]

- Born in Budapest, Hungary, Leo Szilard earned his doctorate in physics from the University of Berlin and taught there until 1933. Szilard left Germany because of anti-Semitic discrimination policies of the Nazis that curtailed the work and advancement of Jewish academics.

  Szilard is known as the principal contributor to the letter sent by Albert Einstein to Franklin Roosevelt, alerting the President to the potential enormous power of a bomb based on uranium fission and Germany's apparent progress toward bomb development. He worked in Chicago with Enrico Fermi as a member of the Manhattan Project. After the war, Szilard devoted much of the rest of his career arguing against the use of atomic energy in weapons of war.[15]

- J. Robert Oppenheimer was the civilian head of Manhattan Project and Director of the Los Alamos Laboratory in New Mexico. He had been selected for the leadership position by General Leslie Groves.

The development and deployment of the bombs that ended the War with Japan cost the U.S. Government more than two billion dollars. As a result of his leadership, Robert Oppenheimer became known as the "father of the atomic bomb." He later served as the first Chairman of the General Advisory Committee of the U.S. Atomic Entergy Commission.

Oppenheimer opposed the development of the hydrogen fusion bomb and eventually lost his security clearance due to purported earlier association with known communists. In 1947, he became Director of the Institute for Advanced Study at Princeton University. Robert Oppenheimer died in 1967. [16]

CITED REFERENCES

[1] http://www.holocaustforgotten.com/
nordhausen.htm

[2] Ken Stone, Editor, *Triumphant We Fly:
A 381st Bomb Group Anthology 1943 – 1945*
(Paducah, Kentucky: Turner Publishing
Company, 1994)

[3] http://en.wikipedia.org/wiki/Mittelbau-Dora

[4] http://www.daviddarling.info/
encyclopedia/P/Paperclip.html

[5] http://en.wikipedia.org/wiki/
Wernher_von_Braun

[6] http://www.russianspaceweb.com/
gorodomlya.html

[7] http://nsarchive.gwu.edu/israel/
documents/reveal/

[8] http://spectrum.ieee.org/telecom/
security/the-real-story-of-stuxnet

9 http://en.wikipedia.org/wiki/Gernot_Zippe

10 www.cnn.com/2011/WORLD/asiapcf/
05/02/bin.laden.timeline/

11 http://www.factcheck.org/2013/02/
rand-pauls-bin-laden-claim-is-urban-myth/

12 http://www.npr.org/2011/09/09/
140333732/in-afghanistan-assessing-
a-rebel-leaders-legacy

13 http://www.history.com/topics/
world-war-ii/george-smith-patton

14 http://www.americanthinker.com/articles/
2012/11/the_mysterious_death_of_gen_
george_s_patton.html

15 http://www.biography.com/people/
leo-szilard-9500919

16 http://www.biography.com/people/
j-robert-oppenheimer-9429168

OTHER REFERENCES

*A Description of the Mittelwerk V-2
Underground Assembly Plant and Mittelbau-
Dora Concentration Camp:*
http://www.subbrit.org.uk/sb-
sites/sites/n/nordhausen/index.shtml

*On Deployment of V-2 Rockets Launched from
The Hague:* http://www.v2platform.nl/book/
V2book_contents.html

*Non-British Personnel in the RAF during the
Battle of Britain:* http://en.wikipedia.org/
wiki/Non-British_personnel_in_the_RAF_
during_the_Battle_of_Britain

About the RAF American Eagle Squadrons:
http://en.wikipedia.org/wiki/
Eagle_Squadrons

*Pigeons as Message Carriers during World War
Two:* http://www.americainwwii.com/
articles/pigeons-of-war/

Circumventing U.S. Neutrality Law:
http://www.afhso.af.mil/shared/media/docu
ment/AFD-100928-005.pdf

Peenemünde Army Research Center:
http://en.wikipedia.org/wiki/Peenem%C3%B
Cnde_Army_Research_Center

*The V-2 was the World's First Long-range
Guided Ballistic Missile:*
http://en.wikipedia.org/wiki/V-2_rocket

*World War II German Army Ranks and
Insignia:* http://en.wikipedia.org/wiki/World_
War_II_German_Army_ranks_and_insignia

*The Morgenthau Plan for Occupation and
Restoration of Germany after World War II:*
http://en.wikipedia.org/wiki/Morgenthau_Pla
n#JCS_1067

The History Place™ World War II in Europe:
http://www.historyplace.com/worldwar2/tim
eline/ww2time.htm

*History and Description of V-2 Rocket
Development at Mittelwerk:*
http://www.v2rocket.com/start/
chapters/mittel.html

The Stuxnet Computer Worm:
http://en.wikipedia.org/wiki/Stuxnet

Life of General George S. Patton:
http://en.wikipedia.org/wiki/
George_S._Patton

Robert Goddard: American Father of Rocketry:
http://www.space.com/19944-robert-
goddard.html

*The Manhattan Project – an Interactive History
(U.S. Department of Energy – Office of History
and Heritage Resources):*
https://www.osti.gov/manhattan-project-
history/index.htm

*A History and Description of the Zippe-type Gas
Centrifuge for Uranium Isotope Separation:*
http://en.wikipedia.org/wiki/Zippe-
type_centrifuge

A Fact Sheet on the Iranian Nuclear Program:
https://www.clarionproject.org/sites/default/
files/Iranian-Nuclear-Program.pdf

*A History of Iran's Nuclear Technology
Development:* http://www.nti.org/
country-profiles/iran/nuclear/

The Urenco Group Nuclear Fuel Company:
http://en.wikipedia.org/wiki/Urenco_Group

About Ahmad Massoud, the Assassinated Leader of the Northern Alliance in Afghanistan: http://en.wikipedia.org/wiki/Ahmad_Shah_Massoud

ABOUT THE AUTHOR

Thomas Settimi graduated from the Institute of Technology at the University of Minnesota and earned a Master's Degree in Physics from the University of California at Riverside. For much of his professional career he has been engaged in technical writing and engineering for the Department of the Navy and defense-related firms.

Thomas resides in Brookings, Oregon, with his wife, Charlotte.

Interested readers may contact Thomas at tsettimi@gmail.com

OTHER NOVELS BY THOMAS SETTIMI

CONVERGENCE

Paperback (ISBN-13: 978-1419661518)
eBook Edition 2012

The feathery white ribbons in the sky above Adams County, Pennsylvania, were nothing unusual—just the vapor trail evidence of high-flying aircraft that one might see on any day. But for the men on the ground below they were a puzzlement. And no wonder: the year was 1863 and the men were Confederate soldiers marching toward the most significant battle of the American Civil War.

Thousands of miles away and 105 years later, Navy pilot Nathaniel Booth and his navigator complete their air mission over Laos and are headed back to the deck of the *USS Enterprise* when their aircraft mysteriously vanishes. Our hero Booth is declared Missing in Action. Years later when Rose Booth, the family matriarch, learns that her son may not have been a casualty of the war as previously believed, she enlists a prominent history professor and his protégé to uncover the truth.

In this carefully researched historical novel with a cosmic twist, the author traces the convoluted struggle to weave together the threads of a lost airman's life and bring solace to a grief-stricken mother.

ROSWELL 1947

Paperback (ISBN-13: 978-0615829173)
eBook Edition 2013

After helping solve the very strange case of a Vietnam-era pilot caught up in a cosmic disruption in time and space as described in the author's novel *CONVERGENCE*, Professor Roger Atwood and Amanda Marshall are off on a new quest. In 1947, Colonel Dieter Hedrick was a young lieutenant serving in the Public Information Office at Roswell Army Air Field, New Mexico. As one of the last surviving witnesses to the strange events that occurred in July of that year, he calls upon investigative reporter, Amanda Marshall, to tell his story of the Roswell Incident.

Upon hearing the Colonel's compelling, yet incomplete, account of the events that occurred more than sixty years ago, Amanda enlists the assistance of Professor Roger Atwood to settle the issue once and for all. Were we really visited by aliens? Was there a government cover-up? In this fast-paced novel based on the often-told story and speculation surrounding the

Roswell Incident, the author presents a startling alternative explanation for one of the most controversial events of the last century.

BEAK OF THE TURTLE

Paperback (ISBN-13: 978-0692210802)
eBook Edition 2014

They came from the stars—from a place in the night sky known to the ancients as the "Beak of the Turtle." They came to Earth in search of their roots and found a civilization that had just begun to stir.

In 1953 Professor Tsum Um Nui was employed as an instructor and researcher in the Anthropology Department at Beijing University. At the urging of a colleague, the professor embarked on a challenging task: translating microscopic symbols engraved on a few ancient stone burial discs. The discs—eventually known as "Dropa Stones"—were discovered by his colleague during a 1938 expedition to the Bayan Har Mountains near the China-Tibet border.

Despite the astonishing nature of his findings, Professor Tsum earned little acclaim for his work; first due to the stifling repression of the Cultural Revolution and later when his findings were deemed to be inconsistent with the philosophy and image of the Chinese Communist Government.

More than fifty years later, the Professor's daughter seeks the assistance of investigators Roger Atwood and Amanda Marshall *(CONVERGENCE and ROSWELL 1947)* to document the life's work of her father and restore his blemished reputation.

Beak of the Turtle is a story of ancient aliens and the quest of modern day investigators to find and interpret the evidence they left behind 4,600 years ago.

BEYOND 2020: A story of liberty lost, hope and recovery

Paperback (ISBN-13: 978-1074544676)
eBook Edition 2019

No one could have predicted it.

After a successful first term, the Trump administration looked forward to winning re-election and moving on to four more years of service to the country and her people.

What, then, could possibly have derailed the President's plan, denying him what was believed to be an assured victory in November 2020?

"Elections have consequences," we are reminded. In the months and years that followed, the voices of Talk Radio sounded the warning that the New Socialism would methodically suppress the freedoms promised in the Constitution, but it would take an America at the brink of revolution to restore what was lost.

Published 16 months before the 2020 presidential election, this fictional account has proved to be amazingly prophetic regarding the current state of politics in America.